I0585437

# MICROMIUM
## CLEAN ENERGY FROM MARS

# MICROMIUM
## CLEAN ENERGY FROM MARS

---

AN ILLUSTRATED NOVELLA BY
# DAVID GITTLIN

www.davidgittin.com

Entelligent Entertainment, LLC

Copyright © 2018, David B Gittlin.
All rights reserved. The use of any part of this publication,
reproduced, transmitted in any form or by any means, electronic,
mechanical, photocopying, recording or otherwise stored in a
retrieval system, without the prior consent of the publisher
is an infringement of the copyright law.

*Micromium* is a work of fiction. Names, characters, places,
and incidents are the product of the author's imagination or appear
in the story fictitiously. Any resemblance to actual persons,
living or dead, and events or certain locales is entirely coincidental.

Diane Donovan, editor
J Caleb Clark, cover design, www.jcalebdesign.com
David Moratto, interior design, www.davidmoratto.com

Published in the United States by
Entelligent Entertainment, LLC

ISBN: 978-0-9882635-4-3

*For Danielle,*
*the light of my life*
———

# CONTENTS

# MICROMIUM
## CLEAN ENERGY FROM MARS

# PROLOGUE

## Television City, California
### August 2033

"GOOD MORNING AND welcome to the Kantor Report. I'm Adam Kantor, bringing you the day's most pressing issues with in-depth coverage from reporters and experts from around the globe.

"In this morning's lead story, domestic and overseas financial markets reacted in turmoil when the US Department of Health and Human Welfare issued air quality warnings in New York, Los Angeles, Chicago and three other major metropolitan cities across the country.

"Joining me from Los Angeles is Cameron Turner. Cameron teaches Environmental Sciences at UCLA and he is the author of the best-selling novel, 'Environmental Armageddon.' Thanks for getting up so early to join us, Professor."

"Good to be here, Adam."

"Professor, you've been an outspoken critic of the government's failure to adequately address the issues of air pollution and global warming. What's wrong with our energy policies?"

"Well, we can't keep building sea walls and counting exclusively on wind, solar, and electric energy to solve the serious environmental problems we're facing. It's true that the world is less dependent on fossil fuels than it's ever been, but until we can end our dependence on oil, coal and natural gas, our biosphere will increasingly be in peril. We must develop a clean energy alternative to fossil fuel now. I stress the word *now*. We can no longer accept the slow rate of change without inviting an environmental meltdown, as my novel suggests. It isn't just the air and the seas. Nature is striking back at us with killer storms. Farmers can't grow their crops due to sudden cold snaps and droughts. Arable land is shrinking. Deserts are expanding. Temperatures keep rising. Air mass flows like the Gulf Stream are changing. We've already seen instances of food rationing, famine and insect-borne epidemics. These effects will intensify and become irreversible if we keep doing business as usual. It's obvious that more money and more effort *must* go into research."

"Thank you, Professor. Also, with us tonight is Jeremy Kornbluth, Vice President of the World Energy Council. Welcome to the show, Mr. Vice President."

"Thanks, Adam, and please call me Jeremy."

"All right, Jeremy. What do you have to say in response to Professor Turner's comments?"

"I can assure you that the WEC is working very hard to decrease the use of fossil fuels and encourage governments and scientists in every country of the world to come up with solutions to these nagging problems. We're discussing legislation that would ban the manufacture of gas and hybrid cars with the United States, England, Korea, and Japan, but as you can imagine, it's just not a step everyone is willing to take."

"By 'everyone' do you mean the major oil producing countries and car makers?"

"Yes. The major oil producers and energy companies have not been innovative enough because it's not in their interests to do so. This leaves industrialized countries in a bind. Without a viable alternative to fossil fuels, they keep polluting the environment to sustain their economies and way of life while simultaneously endangering their quality of life."

"Then what hope can you offer us, Jeremy?"

"I can tell you there is great hope. We're working on a very promising possibility."

"Does it have anything to do with the ore samples from Mars?"

"I don't want to add to the speculation that's been bandied about in the press. I *can* say we're working very hard and hope to have an announcement soon."

"Thank you, Mr. Vice President. We'll follow-up with you on this important developing story."

# Chapter 1
# MOJAVE DESERT

June 2035

"THIS IS TRIAL EIGHTEEN," Kate Blackstone announced. "Testing five one hundredths kilogram of enriched X435.

*"X" for unknown.*

In a forgotten corner of the Mojave Desert, twelve hundred miles away from the control facility where Kate sat, a robotic arm lowered a titanium cylinder into the core of a miniaturized reactor. No humans manned the fully automated testing facility—for good reason.

Six scientists, including Jeremy Kornbluth, observed the test on a seventy- two-inch plasma screen. Kate sat in the middle of them with Vice President and CEO Kornbluth to her left. He had flown in with the WEC science team to monitor and report on the progress of the testing. She recalled one of their conversations from earlier in the day.

"I'm really feeling like today is the day," the WEC Vice President had confided.

She was beginning to feel like Mel Fisher, the legendary treasure hunter, who used to say the same thing for years until he finally found the wreckage of Our Lady of the Atocha; a Spanish Galleon that sank in a hurricane somewhere off the Florida Keys bearing treasure worth hundreds of millions of dollars. Finding the Atocha was only the beginning of Fisher's struggle to capitalize on the sunken treasure. He had to excavate the valuable artifacts and then fight the State of Florida for ownership rights.

The discovery of an unusual ore sample by NASA astronauts during the first manned mission to Mars had been only the beginning of Kate's struggle. She had been selected and tasked by the World Energy Council to harness the power of a substance whose composition did not match any element in the Periodic Table. To say that the task was hard was an understatement. Failure had become the norm. The only progress had been in the degree of failure. The first trial had blown up the testing facility.

Her mother's words echoed in her head. *Girls don't become scientists, Katie. Why don't you choose a nice profession like nursing?*

At times like this, she wondered why she hadn't taken her mother's advice.

"Initiating fission sequence."

Five minutes passed.

"Reaction stable."

Thirty minutes passed with very little conversation in the room. Kate took shallow breaths, as if breathing too hard might upset the delicate miracle occurring in the heart of the reactor. This was the first trial that had lasted more than eight minutes.

"Reaction remains stable," Kate reported. "Material shows no discernable signs of decay. Energy signature remains non-radioactive."

"No radioactive residue *and* an incredibly slow burn rate," Jeremy Kornbluth said. "Remarkable."

"We won't know if the reaction is clean until we can burn the material longer," Kate remarked. "*So far*, all of our tests indicate the subtle emissions are benign."

"I've read every word of your excellent reports, Katie. I remain hopeful that X435 will become the clean energy source we've been searching for to replace fossil fuels."

A minute later an alarm sounded. Lights inside the test chamber flashed red.

"Reaction unstable. Shutting down."

Kornbluth broke the post-trial silence. "Obviously, this trial is a major step forward. And it couldn't have come at a better time with yours truly and my associates in the audience."

Kate laughed dutifully.

"I feel strongly that the council will continue your funding."

Kate concealed her doubts from Kornbluth and the WEC science team. She wondered if her team would ever find the elusive mix of materials and process to safely burn X435. Would they ever find the treasure? Was the mysterious ore one of the most important discoveries in human history—or was it fool's gold?

"Can you do me a favor, Mr. Vice President?"

"Anything Katie."

"Please call me Kate. I hate being called Katie."

Kornbluth's mouth dropped open.

"I have another favor to ask."

"You aren't shy."

"No, sir. If we do pull this off, I'd like to go to Mars to study the crater where they found the ore."

"You want to unlock the energy potential of X435 *and* solve the mystery of the Martian crater's origin. You *are* ambitious, aren't you?

"I suppose so."

"Apply to NASA. I'm sure your qualifications as both a Geologist and Physicist will get you into the training program. Then we'll find out if you have what it takes to be an astronaut. But let's not get ahead of ourselves."

"I tend to do that. Hopefully, we'll learn how to control the reaction soon. Then the engineers will figure out how to build a life-size reactor."

"That's the drill."

"I think you just made a pun, sir."

Kornbluth chuckled and then resumed his serious expression. "We have a long way to go before you or anyone bores test holes to probe the mysteries of the giant Martian crater. We have to make X435 a practical alternative to fossil fuels before it's too late."

# Chapter 2

# ELON MUSK SPACE CENTER

## Houston, Texas
### August 2036

BENJAMIN CALIPHAS WATCHED the launch through a closed-circuit television connection piped into the corner office of his supervisor, Carl Haynes. He had been monitoring the countdown by radio from his office a few floors down since four-thirty in the morning. Haynes, the CEO of the Courtland Aerospace Corporation, had called him upstairs to watch the launch a half-hour before the scheduled liftoff. Watching the launch alone with his boss made Benjamin feel important. He liked to feel important.

Haynes was nervous. It was obvious to Benjamin. It was not hard to figure why he was fidgety. Courtland had been selected by NASA to do the mining feasibility studies on Mars. Courtland had agreed to pay eighty percent of the cost of the mission. If the studies showed promise, the WEC had agreed to award a mineral mining contract to Courtland with a potential value of trillions of dollars. NASA and the other WEC member nations had put up the remaining billions needed to finance the mining studies mission. That's the way business was done in 2036. Share the risk. Governments holding hands. The richest countries in the world had precious little money for space exploration and just about everything else more down to Earth.

The participating nations had something to lose, but a lot more to gain. That was the simple logic Benjamin had used to champion the project. Unfortunately, Benjamin had a lot more to lose than anyone else on the corporate side. He risked standing backwards before a firing squad with his pants down if the Mars mining project didn't pan out. Someone besides the top dogs had to face the music for failure.

Haynes was normally a talker. He had not spoken a word for ten minutes. Benjamin almost felt sorry for him. They listened to the chatter inside the Orion Crew Module. The crew sounded chipper for a group that was about to get punched in their collective guts with eight and a half million pounds of thrust from the three Delta rocket boosters poised for liftoff.

"Initiation of fuel fill sequence confirmed, the Flight Engineer said."

"This is Capcom. We have a message from President Wilbourn. He wishes you, and I quote, 'Godspeed and good hunting. Every citizen of our planet whose heart beats true sends prayers for your safety and a successful mission.'"

"If one more government leader wishes us 'Godspeed' I'm going to barf," the Flight Engineer said on a secured frequency.

Benjamin had watched the Orion crew members interviewed by Kelli Connors, a celebrity reporter, a few weeks before the launch. The crew had been hand-selected by Courtland Aerospace. Under the terms of the deal, NASA trained the crew, but they worked for and were paid by Courtland. The four crew members and their special drilling rig were going to test the sites where robot probes had found traces of the ore scientists had recently named Micromium. The team's surveys would determine if there was enough ore near the surface of Mars to make a mining venture commercially feasible.

Benjamin watched his boss lean back, then forward, then sideways as the countdown continued.

"Relax, Carl. Remind yourself that a kilo of Micromium will power a metropolitan city for an entire year. A few grains of it will power most cars for at least that long. Gas and electric cars will become dinosaurs."

"I wish I could think of that instead of all of the things that can go wrong."

"We've already gotten our money's worth in advertising and goodwill. And our cost is one fifth of the numbers the media is throwing around. They're using the exorbitant costs we normally charge the government on other projects. We're heroes before the fact."

"I liked this project from the moment we started talking about it, Benjamin. Boundless, clean energy produced inexpensively—the answer to the energy crisis—how the hell could anyone not love it? I sold the project—your project—to the boys upstairs. I'm a great salesman and I sell great ideas, but I get nervous when it's time for ideas to make their way in the world. That's when the honeymoon ends. Now we have to sit around with stomach cramps and sleep loss while we wait for the survey results."

"I know it's uncomfortable, but that's why you have me. Let me do the worrying for you. If they find enough ore up there, we're going to get back two thousand times what we invest. I pushed the plasma drive development. We've had more time to perfect the technology than our competitors. We can put people on Mars twice as fast and more safely than our competition. And with our re-usable rocket technology, the mining operation will be highly cost effective."

"And you'll be the man we tap to run the new division. We already have the name: Martian Mining Interplanetary."

"Not tremendously original, but definitely serviceable. And let's not forget that there are other rare minerals up there, like Deuterium. We're getting in on the ground floor of a new business with vast potential."

"You're preachin' to the choir, my boy."

"And you love it."

They watched the pre-launch routine wind down to the final thirty seconds.

"This is Capcom. You are clear for ignition."

To Benjamin, it sounded so matter-of-fact. Of course, it was supposed to sound that way. Let's stay calm. We're just making history here. Maybe changing the course of human existence. But let's not get too excited. Riding into space on top of a multi-stage beast with thousands of moving parts is really no big deal.

The huge Delta engines roared to life. The nineteen-story spacecraft rumbled upward off the launching pad on a fiery cloud exploding underneath it.

They watched the Orion five vehicle ascend noisily into the heavens. Benjamin leaned back in his chair with his fingers forming a steeple in front of his face. His forefingers clicked against each other like mirror image Morse code keys. It was something he did when his emotions got the better of him. He did not berate himself for showing his emotions under the circumstances. So many things depended upon so many other things. He pushed this thought from his mind. Challenges lay ahead. He welcomed the challenges and the unknown. He believed in himself and the technology Courtland Aerospace had developed under his leadership. He knew how to navigate the rapids of big business. He was a man of destiny. He envisioned his bright future manifesting as naturally and inevitably as tomorrow's sunrise.

# Chapter 3

# MARS—PERSONNEL QUARTERS

NOTHING IN LOGAN Marchant's twenty-nine years of life had prepared him for the loneliness and grandeur of a Martian sunrise. The planet's rock and sand surface glittered an angry red. A thousand meters in the distance, the walls of the massive Siloe Patera crater shrugged off the blanket of night. The question of the massive crater's origins lay shrouded in mystery since its discovery. Many scientists believed Siloe Patera was an extinct volcano, but it could just as easily have been gouged by a huge meteor impact. The rim of the crater measured some forty by thirty kilometers. A meteor large enough to create such a crater might have been responsible for the loss of an Earth-like atmosphere on Mars billions of years ago. Similarly, if Siloe Patera marked the grave of an extinct super-volcano, the amount of gas and dust released into the atmosphere might have literally blown the planet's life-supporting atmosphere away. NASA expected Logan and his team to find the answer to these questions. The WEC had more important questions they wanted answered.

The team had two primary directives. Their first task involved the investigation of two deaths caused by a micro meteor shower near the surface rim of the mine. The world and its governments needed closure on the tragic incident. They wanted enhanced safety precautions to prevent more accidents.

The highest priority, however, required the team to audit the subcontractor's mining operation. The WEC wanted the team to estimate the potential ore yield. The mining corporation claimed it was difficult to make accurate yield projections. Martian Mining Interplanetary had also refused to spend resources investigating the origin of the Siloe Patera crater. In their press releases, MMI made the point repeatedly that it was their job to mine the ore and not to do scientific research.

Back home, the sun brought life-sustaining energy and warmth to every living thing. Without the slightest hint of judgment, the sun made life, in all its diverse forms, possible. There was evidence that the sun had once nurtured life on Mars to an infinitely greater extent than it did now. The maps of the planet which Logan had studied depicted ample evidence of plains that might once have been teeming oceans and ravines that might once have been rushing rivers or canals. Manned and unmanned expeditions to Mars had found microbiological life beneath the planet's surface. Scientists speculated that the microbiological evidence represented the vestiges of complex life forms that once thrived on Mars billions of years ago.

While the debate about the history of life on Mars continued, one fact remained: human beings now lived on the planet's surface. Martian Mining Interplanetary, a subsidiary of the Courtland Aerospace Corporation, had established a mining colony on Mars after securing a lucrative mining contract sanctioned by the World Energy Council.

Although he dreamed of commanding deep space exploration missions, Logan could not imagine signing up for seven-year tours of duty like the Martian mining colonists had. Spending years in a state of suspended animation was okay. Just don't ask him to stay in one place for too long. Somehow, he knew that if he didn't die flying in space, he'd live to an advanced age on Mother Earth, hopefully surrounded by loving family members and fond memories of glorious extra-terrestrial adventures that advanced the cause of his species.

He had a long way to go in the loving family department. For starters, his relationship with his Air Force Colonel prick of a father was a lost cause. If the man had any love in him, it was as hard to find as a puddle of water on the arid planet he stared out at through the porthole of his living quarters. He often wondered if his mother's highly premature death from a brain tumor had resulted from an unconscious death wish she developed from the certain knowledge that the man she'd married would never make her happy. The wishy-washy woman his father married after her death, he suspected from early on, hung around only because she had no better place to go. His hatred of his father led Logan to change his last name to his natural mother's maiden name when he reached the age of twenty-one.

His upbringing left him with an empty hole in his soul that nothing filled, no matter how hard he tried. The deep dark pit of emptiness inside him was too painful to experience for more than a few seconds. If he stayed too long, it felt like the dark place would drag him down like some dinosaur that suffocated horribly in the La Brea tar pits millions of years ago.

He had barely spoken to his older sister, Stephanie, since leaving home for UCLA. She dreamed of supporting herself as a freelance photographer while earning a living as part-time graphic artist and high-end prostitute. How he and his sister had issued from the same parents remained a baffling mystery. He worried that Stephanie's black sheep lifestyle might someday cast a shadow over his career and lofty ambitions. Thus, he kept his distance from a sister who never listened to his advice anyway.

With no wife, girlfriend, or children, Logan had nothing to come home to. Someday he might find satisfying and lasting relationships. It might happen much later in life, when he had the luxury of time and circumstances to clear the emotional wreckage of his childhood and adolescence. Until then, he focused only on his career path and the job at hand.

His watch chimed. The time had arrived for his breakfast briefing with the audit team. Now began the regrettable business of investigating two tragic deaths and the spadework required to compile a comprehensive report on the Mars mining operation.

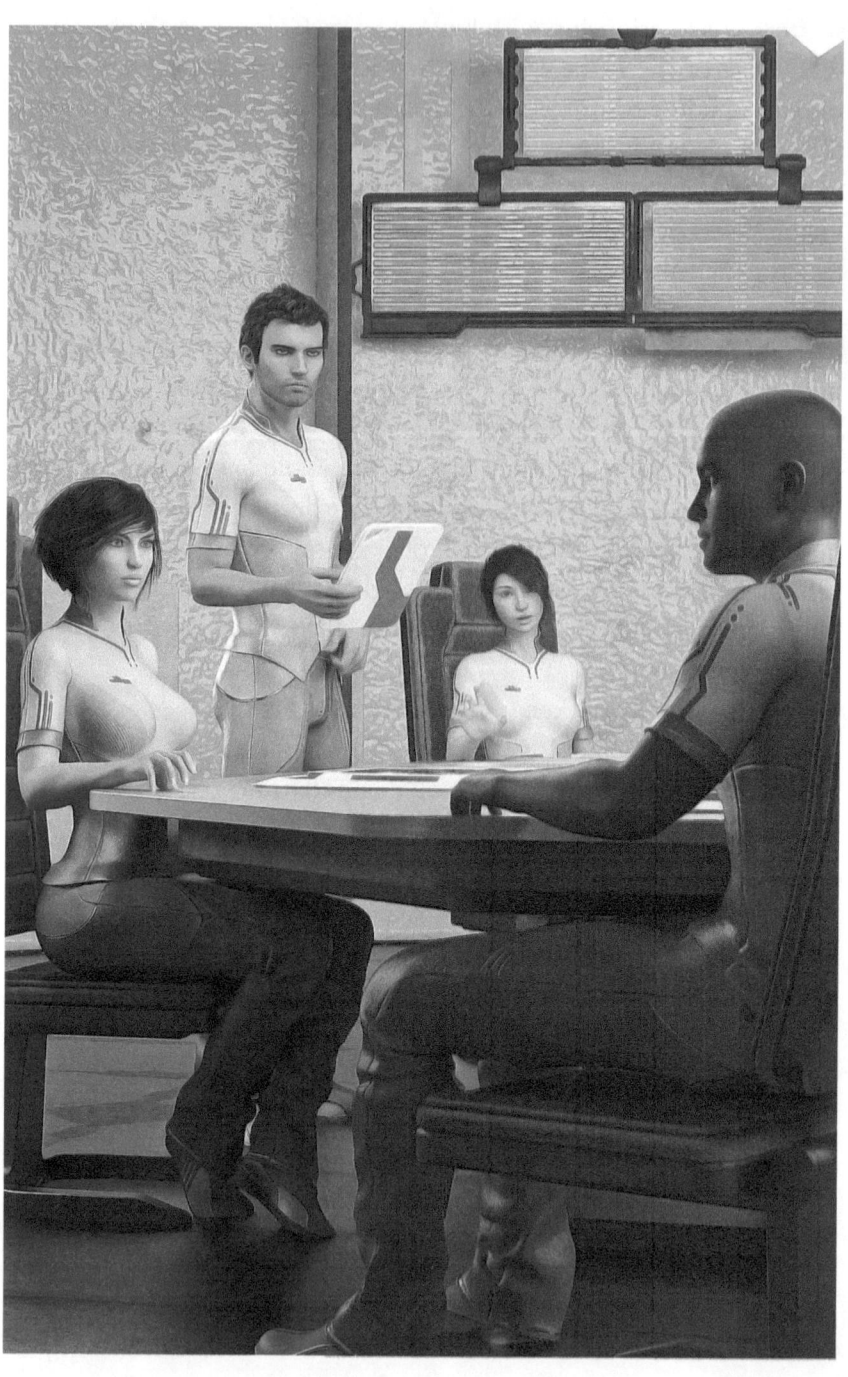

# Chapter 4

# MARS—BREAKFAST BRIEFING

IF NOT FOR the technology developed for the Mars One mission, Logan would not be sitting at a breakfast table surrounded by the uncommon members of his audit team.

The Mars One mission represented mankind's first attempt to plant a colony on another world. The Mars One colonists had arrived five years before the Martian mining colony existed. Twenty brave souls had committed themselves to living out their lives on Mars. The media closely followed their stories. The Mars One mission exemplified some of the most noble human impulses: curiosity and the quest for knowledge and new frontiers. It sprang from the necessity of learning how to live on another world in the face of deteriorating environmental conditions on Earth.

It had taken decades to develop the technology required to build the spacecraft and living facilities. Thousands of details had to be ironed out, including the challenging job of selecting and training the astronaut/colonists. Even with the massive resources of a giant aerospace company like Courtland Aerospace combined with its behemoth joint venture partner, Alexis Energy Systems, the Martian mining venture might never have escaped the gravity of economic risk if the project had started from scratch. While the Mars One pioneers lived and worked hundreds of kilometers away on this starkly beautiful and mostly desolate planet, the mining operation pulled a miraculous ore out of the Martian underground.

As was the case with many of the watershed events of human history, Logan mused, the discovery of Micromium was an accident. When irradiated during a routine test, a small fragment cut from a rock sample found near the Siloe Patera crater blew up a robotic lab. Fortunately, two yards of insulating concrete and steel had saved the engineers and scientists performing the test from injury. For safety's sake, NASA and the WEC moved all subsequent testing to a fully automated facility in the Mojave Desert with no humans around for hundreds of miles.

Logan felt proud to have Kate Blackstone, the woman who was primarily responsible for harnessing the ore's potential, as one of the audit team members. The small quantities needed to generate long-lasting, exponential power had inspired scientists to name the ore Micromium. Its atomic structure included elements foreign to any of the elements in the Periodic Table, the building blocks of every substance known to mankind. The unorthodox composition of Micromium made it virtually impossible to synthesize.

No radioactive residue from the fusion reaction made this remarkable new energy source even more appealing. This meant no heavy materials cleanup or disposal costs; no environmentally threatening side-effects. No muss and no fuss—just clean, affordable energy. Simply amazing stuff—so amazing it, paid to make the enormous investment to mine the ore on Mars and export it back to Mother Earth.

While every effort had been made to make the recreation room warm and conducive to social intercourse, the limitations of expensive payload space kept the design of the living quarters utilitarian. Someday, extra-terrestrial habitats might resemble the opulent interiors described in the Jules Verne novels Logan had read as a boy.

Phase one of the construction process, however, had focused on the essentials of survival. It consisted of seven inflated domes protected from cosmic radiation by solid rock, known as regolith, blasted from the Martian soil. In time, the mining base would grow as more domes and amenities made by 3-D printing sprang up and rockets from Earth delivered supplies beyond the colonists' manufacturing capabilities. Better living conditions meant higher productivity. Nothing in private enterprise was done without an ulterior motive, Logan had observed; one of the many reasons he would never be happy confined to the shackles of a conventional business career.

The team sat around a small table in comfortable military jumpsuits emblazoned with the Word Energy Council logo. The logo consisted of a realistic photo of the Earth taken from an orbiting spacecraft with the letters WEC stitched across the center in shiny white and gold thread. The slogan "A Clean Energy Future" circled the globe in the color of the sky on a bright summer's day.

Logan could not help noticing the loose-fitting attire did little to hide the alluring figures of Kate Blackstone and Kaneko Fukui. Fate had blessed the team with two beautiful science nerds; Kate, a geologist, and Kaneko, an exobiology specialist and medical doctor.

Both women wore their hair cut boyishly short. Kate's russet hair framed her symmetrical Irish-American features and blazing blue eyes. Her face and expression virtually crackled with energy. Kaneko's wide-set brown eyes often reflected the wonder, awe, and curiosity with which she viewed the world around her. The high forehead hinted at her genius-level intelligence. Kaneko's long, slightly flattened nose and delicate mouth were indicative of her sensitivity.

"I'm waiting for the day when I can make better sushi with the 3-D printer," Kaneko said with a frown. "This tastes a long way from home made."

"Yeah, this is supposed to be steak and eggs with Worcestershire sauce," Rashawn Livingston said, pointing to the meal sitting in the paper tray. "It tastes more like fried catfish seasoned with a dash of tumbleweed."

"Patience, people. You can't expect the printer to nail your requests first shot out of the oven. Give the chef feedback and some time to make adjustments," Logan said.

He liked Rashawn and appreciated his precise style of performing the responsibilities of team navigator, EVA specialist, and co-pilot. His grey eyes sparkled with intelligence and sensitivity; the result of a bookish childhood that put him on the wrong end of cruel jokes from his peers. From their first conversation, Logan detected Rashawn's depth and thoughtfulness. Rashawn's depth, however, never stopped him from poking fun at himself and others.

"I'm enjoying my beet salad with sunflower seeds," Kate said. "Maybe you guys need to become vegetarians like me."

Kaneko made booing sounds while Rashawn acted like he was choking to death.

Logan cocked his head sideways. "It's good to see you guys bonding so nicely, but we have a big day ahead of us. Let's review your priorities one last time. Kate?"

He watched their smiles fade. They had plenty of uncomfortable questions to ask of the Mars mining staff. It was Logan's job to make sure his team got the answers the bureaucrats back home wanted without undermining the morale of the mining staff. The word had come down from the World Energy Council: Do nothing to interrupt the flow of the precious ore back to Earth. The word had become the categorical imperative for the audit team's mission.

As the team leader, Logan was fully versed in the backgrounds of his team. Kate, for instance, had a Doctorate in Geology and a Masters' Degree in Physics. With her academic background, keen interest in the space program, and exceptional athletic skills, Kate fit right in on the audit team. She had beaten out hundreds of other people the WEC had considered for her position on the team, although her height was less than ideal for the cramped passenger quarters of a spacecraft.

Logan also had confidential access to the psychological profiles of his team. He knew, for instance, that Kate's height had been a source of uneasiness and teasing during her prepubescent and teenage years. As she matured, Kate had learned to feel at home with who she was both inwardly and outwardly. There would always be the same doubts and insecurities that assail all of humanity, but Kate Blackstone had an exceptionally even keel for someone relatively new to the space program.

"I tested all of my instruments before daybreak. Everything checks out. No signs of any damage from the landing," Kate reported.

"Course not. You couldn't ask for a better landing," Rashawn said.

"I didn't hear anyone ask," Logan said. "Go on, Kate."

"I'll interview the miners and examine the core samples they've taken to determine the potential of the ore deposit. Then I'll oversee the placement of the pneumatic drill to begin taking our own samples. I'll test the two veins of ore for yield potential and consider the origin of Siloe Patera."

"Excellent, Kate." Logan turned to Kaneko Fukui. "Your turn, Doc."

Kaneko had also impressed Logan from the minute she had shown up for training. Her combination of intelligence, self-confidence, ambition and independence made her stand out in any crowd. After reading Kaneko's resume, Logan assumed he would be introduced to a very serious person when they met for the first time. Logic dictated that someone with a PHD in the study of alien life forms *and* a medical degree had little time or patience for anything but business. To his surprise, Logan found Kaneko maintained a fun-loving and mischievous demeanor. She had her own way of doing things and resisted excessive oversight from superiors, but Logan had never seen her display the kind of arrogance common in others with Kaneko's gifts.

"My first assignment will be to autopsy the bodies of the two accident victims," Kaneko began. "After that, I'll begin cataloguing and examining any life forms that have been turned up by the mining operation. I'll also take one of the rovers and collect samples from the surrounding terrain to test for life forms."

"Thanks, Kaneko."

All eyes now turned to Rashawn Livingston. Character lines etched the regular African-American features of his face. He had the natural physique of an NFL linebacker. The lure of pro sports had tempted him in college, but his childhood dream of becoming an astronaut had kept his career track as direct and true as the courses he plotted on their trip to Mars. Rashawn confided to Logan how hard he had found it to leave the varsity football team to concentrate on his studies. It had been even harder to streamline his bulky body into the svelte shape required to pilot the aircraft he dreamed of flying. He graduated Princeton University as a math major and earned a Master's Degree in Aeronautics while in the Navy. As a Navy pilot, Rashawn flew dangerous combat and reconnaissance missions. He received the Medal of Valor for saving a fellow pilot behind enemy lines. After his distinguished Navy career, NASA accepted Rashawn into its training program for deep space astronauts.

"I'll be checking the mining sites for structural integrity. I'll also be talking to the Operations Manager about the results of their exploration missions for new veins of ore."

"Thanks, Rashawn." Logan addressed the whole group again. "I'm expecting the mining staff to cooperate. If you encounter any blowback, report it to me immediately. I'm reminding you for the umpteenth time that we're not here to ruffle feathers. We're here to politely get answers. We have the court-awarded right to be here. If conflicts arise, keep in mind the courts have decided the interests of billions of people back home outweigh the private interests of Martian Mining Interplanetary. We're here to pierce MMI's corporate veil, but keep them smiling while we do it. In other words, keep your interpersonal skills fully engaged. Am I clear?"

"Does that include sexual favors, Commander?"

"Shut up, Kate."

Logan looked around the table at his team. Like professional athletes, they were all freaks of nature, possessing unique blends of specialized skills, high IQ's, and character. He asked if they had any final questions or comments. No one had any.

"Okay, folks. Let's do this."

# Chapter 5

# MARS—SILOE PATERA MINE

THE PRIMARY MINE site was a cave dug into the north face of the Siloe Patera crater. Kate exited the elevator that had taken her down more than seventeen hundred meters to the crater floor. Siloe Patera, named after the fifteenth century Castilian sculptor and architect Diego Siloé, comprised two craters in one. The mine was situated at the bottom of the deeper crater.

Kate knew that the second part of the crater's name was derived from the Latin word *paterae,* a designation used to describe Martian volcanos that generally exhibited a circular mountainous wall known as a caldera and an empty molten rock enclosure underneath known as a chamber. Siloe Patera's name, of course, involved pure speculation. The crater's physical features tended to support the volcano argument over the meteor impact theory. Only detailed on-site observation and testing by a skilled geologist promised to solve the mystery.

Kate intimately knew the arguments on both sides of the controversy. She knew some of the participants personally. Some scientists thought the Patera type of geological structure and several similar structures in this region of Mars (known as Arabia Terra) were calderas of very flat volcano complexes. These volcanoes resembled the few super-volcanoes on Earth. One such super-volcano located at Yellowstone National Park had a caldera measuring sixty kilometers long and forty kilometers wide. The explosive force of these super-volcanoes equated roughly to the detonation of a fifty-megaton nuclear bomb.

From the white-paper she wrote in undergraduate school, Kate had learned that during their active stages, super-volcanoes form large calderas instead of volcanic cones. Her research revealed that scientists estimated the magma chamber located underneath the complex of volcanoes in the Terra Arabia region had a volume of at least one thousand cubic kilometers; enormous when compared to the average volcano. Eruptions of super-volcanoes on Earth were known to be very rare and none had been observed in recorded history. However, it was commonly known that the effects of super-volcanoes were catastrophic and widespread.

Kate learned that the volcanic region surrounding a super-volcano is lifted over long periods of time by the accumulation of gas in the magma chamber, and that magma emerges in locations distant from the chamber. A circular rift appears around the magma chamber resulting from the uplifting of the ground. The interior of this lid then sinks into the empty magma chamber, leaving behind the caldera typical of a super-volcano.

From her extensive studies of satellite and Martian probe photos, Kate determined that Siloe Patera exhibited some of these characteristics. She also noted that the crater lacked a central mountain in the middle, typical of impact craters; another feature supporting the volcano theory. On the other hand, there were numerous examples of impact craters on Mars whose rims and central mountains had long been eradicated by erosion. Finally, since there were two depressions inside the crater, it was entirely possible that Siloe Patera was both an impact crater *and* a volcano.

Without a doubt, Kate had her work cut out for her. Taking a moment to observe her surroundings, she suddenly felt detached from her circumstances. How surreal it felt to be standing in a massive depression nearly two thousand meters below the surface of Mars.

What drove her to be here? Was it her thirst for scientific knowledge? Was it a need for adventure? Did she have to prove herself worthy to her super-successful father? Was it all of the above?

She knew her father loved her, but he was always off in some distant part of the world building skyscrapers. Growing up with two older brothers had fueled her competitive nature. She recalled playing football with them as a gangly eight-year-old in the backyard of their five-bedroom home in an exclusive neighborhood of Tulsa, Oklahoma. It seemed like only yesterday.

The news of her brother's death had crushed her. Liam, the bravest and wildest of the three, had crashed and died five years ago while testing a prototype jet fighter for the Grumman Corporation. Her oldest and more conservative brother, Corey, had gone into the family engineering business with her Dad, Corwyn Senior. Her mother, Ellyn, approved of Corey's decision to follow in his father's footsteps. Kate's decision to enter Astronaut training had infuriated and horrified her mother. The last thing she wanted was to lose another child. Their already strained relationship had almost snapped when Kate made the announcement. In addition to their differences, millions of miles of cold, dead space now separated them. Like a slap in the face, thoughts of her mother catapulted her back into the present.

The powerful mining drill reminded Kate of a hybrid mechanical dinosaur. The drill assembly resembled the curvilinear body of a Brontosaurus with a long thin neck supporting the head of a Tyrannosaurus Rex. The gnashing teeth of the huge head tore chunks of rock from the wall. Hydraulic pumps sucked rock fragments into the reptilian neck where lasers blasted it into a fine powder. Air pressure forced the powder into the body of the beast where highly calibrated laser sensors directed the separation of precious Micromium ore from the useless sand residue. Finally, the guts of the dinosaur converted the Micromium powder into ingots for transportation to the subterranean refining plant at the bottom of Siloe Patera. The refining plant purified and transformed the Micromium ingots into fuel pellets for the fusion reactors waiting back on Earth.

The robot miner's remarkably human-sounding voice clicked off inside Kate's space helmet. She had the honor of being the first outsider to observe the corporation's secretive mining operation. After video-recording the android's explanation of the process, she swung the camera towards the drill rig assembly.

"I hope you don't intend to video the MX-60." the robot said politely.

"Actually, I do." She kept her tone cordial, following Logan's instructions.

Other than its humanoid shape, Martian Mining Interplanetary had not spent lavishly to make their mining robots look like living, breathing people. From its transparent skull and featureless face down to its six-fingered hands that looked more like claws, the robot's design was purely functional. Kate understood the reason for this. The robots lacked physical appeal because no one besides the programming and maintenance staff of the mining colony needed to interact with them. The robots spent most of their time reliably working underground without complaining and in abject isolation.

"I'm not authorized to allow you to make videos of anything that will compromise the corporation's competitive position."

With its bland tone, the android sounded like a mean sixth grade teacher.

"Oh, my. It seems we have a problem." Kate switched communication channels. "I'm here with this dumb machine, Logan. It won't let me video the mining machinery."

Logan's voice crackled through the earpiece in her helmet. "Move on to your soil experiments. We'll talk to the station manager about this after you return to base."

"Copy that. Too-da-loo," she said to the dour robot miner.

* * *

All the tools Kate needed to gather soil samples from the Siloe Patera crater dangled from the utility belt she wore. In the lower-than-Earth gravity of Mars, the tools barely registered as an extra burden. She had divided the crater into four quadrants. Methodically, Kate gathered surface samples from the first quadrant. On the next visit to the mine, Kate and Rashawn would bring the team's special pneumatic drill to dig deeper for more samples. She and Rashawn would need a rover to gather samples from all four quadrants due to the enormous size of the two depressions. Transporting and positioning the drill represented another set of logistical challenges. It was going to be a laborious and time-consuming process, but at least this was a start.

After an hour of gathering surface samples, Kate carefully labeled each bag of samples and snapped a series of digital photos of the first quadrant. She took a moment to admire the stars shining in the black firmament of the rugged, unfriendly planet named after the Roman god of war. She imagined the mountains and plains teeming with animal and plant life under a cloudless blue sky. Surely, Mars had been a Garden of Eden in the distant past. The topography reminiscent of canals, river beds and long-dead oceans hinted strongly in that direction. For some reason, the Creator, in its wisdom or folly, had withdrawn a life-giving finger from this world, leaving it barren and ruled by dust storms and meteor showers. She hoped human ingenuity might someday terraform Mars back into its former beauty and glory. The possibility beckoned those adventurous souls willing and able to take the gamble.

Enough dreaming. She had plenty of work to do in the here and now. Laden with her samples, Kate began the trek back to the skyscraper elevator, itself a monument to MMI's pioneering technology.

# Chapter 6

# MARS—OPERATIONS ARRAY

THE OPERATIONS MANAGER'S office sat in an open corner of an area known as the "Operations Array." Here, Logan quickly learned, the heart of the mining complex beat at a pace set by the team of three software engineers. They controlled the activity of the robot miners, interior lighting and temperature, life support systems, internal and external communications, and just about every other vital function of the mining base.

When the base was first established, the human staff performed multiple roles. In time, more people arrived to handle the administrative load; and the living quarters, operations center, and recreation centers grew larger. Still, the size of the human mining staff remained relatively small in relation to the scope of the mining operation. Training, transporting, and supporting one staff member on Mars cost MMI upwards of a hundred million dollars. The corporation preferred not to make the exact cost information available to the public. Logan's concern about the staff's careful guarding of what they termed "proprietary information" had begun to grow.

The Operations Manager introduced himself as Oscar Kaminsky. He shook hands with Logan and Kate vigorously. He gave Logan the initial impression of an open and bright man, standing about five-foot-eight inches tall with flaming red hair, keen blue eyes, and pale skin. Logan had noticed the Caucasian members of the staff tended to be unnaturally pale in skin tone. Mars was not a place to go sun bathing.

"Please, have a seat," Kaminsky offered. "Sorry for the lack of privacy. As you can see, square footage is expensive here and we have nothing to hide; at least from each other."

Kaminsky opened one arm to indicate the other staffers in the array.

Logan pretended to be amused by Kaminsky's attempt at humor. "I'm sure you have nothing to hide from us," he countered amiably.

"I'm here to help in any way that I can. I suppose you'll want me to begin by filling you in on the unfortunate accident that led to the deaths of our co-workers."

Logan nodded.

"What can I say to supplement the official report? Let's see." The Operations Manager gripped his chin and narrowed his eyes. "Jesse and Anna went out to repair a mining robot. Our remote cameras showed it had damaged an arm while clearing away debris from the north wall rock face. We allowed Corporal Blackstone to see the MX-60 in action. Don't you think our dual process of mining and refining the ore simultaneously is remarkably economical and efficient?"

"We'll get to the mining process in due course," Kate said. "Let's stay with Anna and Jesse for now."

Logan winced inwardly. Kate's formal tone betrayed her anger over the terse exchange that had occurred with the mining robot.

"Jesse and Anna took one of the rovers to the crater. We always work in pairs outside of the base for safety. Well, the sad fact is that our safety protocols can't prevent freak accidents. A few minutes after leaving the rover on their way to the lift, a shower of tiny meteorites. struck Jesse and Anna. The shower killed them instantly."

"Were there any calls for help?" Logan asked.

"Nothing. Their feeds just went dead. I sent Josh and Gabriel, two of our software engineers, out to see what happened. They found the bodies and brought them back to base. It was horrible. There was nothing we could have done to prevent this from happening."

"Do you have their space suits stored somewhere?" Kate asked.

"We recycled all of the salvageable parts. We recycle almost everything." Kaminsky looked puzzled. "What would you want with their spacesuits?"

"All part of a thorough investigation," Logan said.

"I didn't see any reason to preserve the suits. Jesse and Anna died from asphyxiation due to a loss of suit pressure. We found their bodies frozen solid. We shipped them home for further examination and a proper Earth burial. Like I said, it was a freak accident. The risks here are extreme. You both know this. That's why the pay is outrageous and all our contracts contain a hold harmless clause."

Logan let the question go. "How are you and your people coping with the loss?"

"It's been difficult. Morale was low for weeks after the incident. We've had to spread Anna and Jesse's workload to the other staffers. Jesse did an excellent job with our communications and orbiting satellite support. Anna was primarily in charge of records and documentation. She was also great at her job; a real natural. You don't replace people like those two easily. We'll just have to make do until their replacements arrive."

"So, they were well-liked?"

"Everyone gets along here. We're all very professional."

"Of course," Logan said. "Let's switch gears and talk about access to information. We ran into a bit of a glitch when Kate attempted to video your 'all in one' mining machine. I hope you understand that my team has been granted full access to your operations and records by an interplanetary court order."

"We don't intend to interfere with your work here," Kaminsky said. Logan detected a note of exasperation.

"Then why did your robot miner stop me from doing my job?" Kate asked.

"It's their programming. We haven't had time to reprogram them with the extra work my people have had to shoulder. Just be patient. We'll get around to making the changes necessary to facilitate your investigation."

"I'd appreciate it if you could get around to it sooner than later," Kate said.

Logan glanced at Kate and winked. "Corporal Blackstone has many virtues. One of them is not patience. She's all about getting the job done. She's been known to run over people who get in her way."

Kate looked at the ceiling while shaking her head. "I do not run people over. Robots maybe—not people."

Logan noticed Josh and Gabriel look up from their work with blank expressions, as if they had never heard laughter before.

"At the risk of sounding impatient, are the core samples ready that I requested?" Kate asked with a smirk.

"Again, my apologies. We'll have them ready soon. We have so many priorities and only so much time. We're under tremendous pressure to fulfill our quotas."

"And we have only so much time to spend here, Mr. Kaminsky. I'm sure you realize that," Logan said.

"Of course, of course. Not to worry. We'll have your samples ready; hopefully by tomorrow."

The meeting ended on that somewhat sour note. Logan and Kate left the Operations Array to meet privately in the rec hall where their day had started. Thankfully, they found themselves alone in the room.

"We expected some resistance," Logan said, "but it's more than I anticipated."

"I'm getting the same feeling. It really pisses me off."

"We have to be gently persistent, Kate. It's on us to motivate them to cooperate. We must be nice and polite. Even if it hurts."

"It hurts."

"I know." He felt the urge to take her hand to calm her down. What was up with that? One of the Ten Commandments they operated under was the strict prohibition against inappropriate relationships.

Was his heart feeling the first stirrings of a *verboten* attraction to this woman? The eyes of the dark place inside him opened. *Go back to sleep,* he told it.

"I suppose we could sit here holding hands and feeling sorry for ourselves," she said, "but we have a few mountains to climb."

Was she reading his mind? Shit. "Yeah, let's start climbing." *Climb what? The mountains of work, you idiot.*

# Chapter 7

# MARS—SILOE MINE SITE

RASHAWN PULLED THE rover up to the parking bumper a few hundred meters from the wall of the crater. Letting himself out onto the rust-red Martian soil, he playfully jumped over the median separating the parking area from the path to the funicular. Human ingenuity and perseverance never ceased to amaze him. Somehow, MMI had managed to install two cable cars to ferry miners up and down the mountainous crater wall. From his lifelong interest in things mechanical, Rashawn had learned that the counter-balancing weight of the two cars helped propel them up and down the mountain. Erecting a funicular on Earth was an engineering feat. Erecting one on Mars was just shy of a miracle.

Glancing sideways, he noticed the stakes in the ground outlining the spot where the bodies of Jesse MacMahn and Anna Petrovsky lay before they were recovered. Sadness and a sudden psychic chill overwhelmed him. He felt for the families of the slain duo. The thought of their sudden deaths reminded him of the ever-present dangers he was either brave or foolish enough to face in the hostile environment of outer space and this alien world.

Rashawn looked away from the accident scene to gaze into the heavens above the enormous mouth of the Siloe Patera crater. The stars shone brightly through the thin Martian atmosphere. Somewhere up there, the spirit of his father, Earl, looked down on him.

"Livingston to base. I'm approaching the lift. Will be going silent until I reach the bottom."

"Roger that," a robotic voice from the communications center acknowledged.

He switched off his intercom. His report to base was a bit of a lie. He needed a little extra time for himself and someone else.

Rashawn kept walking and looking up. "Hello, Daddy," he said to the stars. "How you doin' up there? I hope you're happy. I feel you takin' care of us like you did when you were here. Not here on Mars. You know what I mean. I miss you every day. We all miss you. The family is doing fine. I guess you know that. You taught me and Deshawn right. We'll never forget you. We all love you."

On the ride up the crater wall, Rashawn wondered where he and his twin brother, Deshawn, would be today without Earl Livingston. They had been "two holy terrors" as little boys, his mother never failed to remind him. They certainly wouldn't have made it this far in life without the emotional and financial support his parents had provided. Most of all, his father, Earl.

At the top of the wall, he crossed a short concrete sidewalk to the lift entrance. They called it a lift instead of an elevator. Maybe because it wasn't an elevator. It was more like a moving platform large enough to accommodate up to twenty people — or people and robots. It was exciting to be making his first descent into the depths of Siloe. Siloe had become the foreshortened name of the Siloe Patera crater among his friends. He thought of the other members of the audit team as his friends. They had spent a month training together before the liftoff, and then three months in tight quarters on the journey to Mars. There was nothing like the crucible of three months in space packed together like baked beans in a can to forge friendships or create animosity.

Fortunately, he got along with everyone. He even liked them. It seemed the others felt the same way towards him and towards each other. He had learned that this camaraderie was in part engineered by psychological screening intended to assemble a team of compatible personalities. As with all aspects of space exploration, as little as possible was left to chance, even when it came to the dynamics of human relationships.

Rashawn had a hunch the audit team would need each other as much for survival on Mars as they did in outer space.

To his surprise, a robot miner met him in the lift.

"I am here to escort you down to the mine," it said.

The lift jerked as it started down. Rashawn grabbed the safety railing for support. The robot's gold alloy and aluminum body fascinated him. It was the first time he had been this close to one of them.

"You guys figured I couldn't find the big old mine on my own?"

"I am not programmed to answer this question."

"Too bad they didn't program you with a sense of humor."

He stared at the wall of the crater through the wire mesh of the enclosure. The red stripes of soil, interspersed with gray frozen smectite clay, reminded him of the colorful rock formations he'd seen on one of his rare vacations in Sedona, New Mexico.

He listened to the whining sound coming from the powerful engine sitting atop the steel beams crowning the lift shaft. Three thick cables connected the lift to wheels churning directly below the engine chassis. The sound of the engine grew fainter the lower they went. *Just three cables and a cranky robot separating me from eternity,* Rashawn thought. He looked up. There was nothing but black emptiness overhead.

"Follow me," the robot said when the lift door opened at the bottom of the crater.

Lighting fixtures placed strategically along Siloe's floor illuminated the path to the mine. The round lights, about three feet in diameter, were mounted on tripods. Rashawn had studied the architectural and engineering drawings prepared for the mine construction. It fascinated him to learn that the recently installed solar cells stored enough energy to power the lights for up to ten hours straight. As he passed each fixture, the lights began to resemble one-eyed mechanical monsters. The techs had shut down the mining operation temporarily to accommodate his inspection. Working practically alone and this far beneath the surface was beginning to affect him. He had read about deep sea divers experiencing hallucinations. He reminded himself to stay sharp and frosty. This was no big deal. It was just a routine inspection.

The robot's presence began to annoy him. Something told him the thing had an agenda beyond simply looking out for his safety. The feeling could easily be paranoia born of "the deep-sea effect." It made sense not to be down here alone, but he also craved the freedom to explore and inspect without the feeling of being watched.

"I'll go in alone. Please wait for me here," Rashawn requested politely, remembering Logan's instructions. The requirement included a polite demeanor towards the robotic as well as the human members of the mining staff.

The robot acted like it didn't hear the request. "Please watch your step in the mine. Avoid stepping on the tracks."

They reached the entrance to the main mining site. Clearly, the robot was programmed to baby-sit him every step of the way. He might as well get used to it.

Engineers had assembled the drill rig piece by piece at the location where the drilling began. As the rig ate into the side of the crater, more tracks were added to facilitate the movement of the ponderous machine. From where Rashawn stood, the mine looked to be cut about two hundred meters into the crater wall.

As they entered the mine, Rashawn unclipped the flashlight from his utility belt. He appreciated the unique opportunity to see the mining operation first hand. Inspecting the buttressing structure of a mining tunnel normally wasn't a job that brought the blood to a boil. In this situation; it did.

He began checking the support beams. They had been manufactured on Mars. Creating building materials *in-situ* was a big deal, Rashawn had learned in training. Mars, unlike Earth's moon, was rich in mineral deposits that enabled the colonists to manufacture plastics, ceramics, aluminum, and steel, as well as other vital products. Manufacturing *in-situ* saved time and money and would soon open the door to the possibility of larger settlements on Mars. In the not-too-distant future, people would be able to move their families to Mars, shop in a mall, work, play, pursue happiness to the fullest, and die with a smile. That was the general idea, anyway. And here walked Rashawn Livingston, a brave pioneer paving the way for all of this to happen. Saving Earth's environment was the first step, and Rashawn was proud to be playing a key role. *I sure am one important dude*, he thought, and laughed to himself.

He kept walking, sweeping his flashlight over the steel beams, searching for stress fractures or improper construction. *Everything looks fine,* he thought, while listening to his breathing inside his super-strong, temperature controlled, gadget-packed spacesuit. Nothing like the toasty feeling inside of a cutting-edge spacesuit when walking around in sub-zero temperatures.

His flashlight beam fell on a metal door cut in the rock face to the immediate left of the hulking drill rig.

Rashawn moved towards the door. The robot scuttled along by his side. "I need to get in there. Is it locked?"

"I am not authorized to open it," The robot said.

"What's behind the door?"

"I am not authorized to answer this question."

He turned to the robot in disbelief. "What?"

"You are not authorized to go in there."

"I am authorized to go anywhere I damn please."

"Not in there." The robot reached out. Its six-fingered claw closed around his wrist.

Although it stood only five feet, smaller than most men, the robot had suddenly transformed into a frightening presence.

"Let go of me." Rashawn had half a mind to rip his arm from the machine's grip to show it who was boss. But then his suit might rip and he would die. So that was not such a great idea.

"I said, let go of my arm."

Gripping his wrist, the robot seemed to be considering what to do next.

"You will not go in there."

"Are you going to stop me?"

"I will stop you if necessary."

"I can't fucking believe this."

Now it was his turn to decide what to do next. He was too far down to communicate with the base. "All right, shithead. I'll finish my inspection and report this bullshit to my team leader."

He had stepped over the politeness boundary by a thousand miles. He found that he didn't care. The thing had no right to be holding onto him.

"And I hope they fry your ass for this," he added for good measure.

Finally, the robot let go.

"Son of a bitch," Rashawn breathed aloud. "Wait 'til Logan hears about this."

# Chapter 8

# EARTH—MMI HEADQUARTERS

BENJAMIN CALIPHAS EXAMINED the intricate scale model of the second phase of the mining colony mounted on a pedestal in front of his desk. Ricardo Ortiz, the lead designer on the project, stood behind the model.

"As you can see, sir, the three domes are strategically placed in a triangle and connected by spacious tunnels to allow for the movement of materials and machinery as well as pedestrian traffic. The first dome is a multi-level living quarters with larger apartments on the top floor."

"Who are the larger apartments for?"

"I imagine there will be a steady stream of MMI executives and WEC representatives visiting the base."

Ortiz indicated a bank of apartments on the top floor, visible through the cutaway view. "We've allocated several apartments for them here, sir. In time, we may need extended-stay housing for MMI executives as the base grows. I'm assuming additional ore site discoveries."

"Excellent."

"The second dome houses our manufacturing facilities and the third dome will be a greenhouse for growing food. Now, the manufacturing—"

"—I've read and reviewed the design documents thoroughly," Benjamin interrupted. "You and your team have thought of everything, including a spa where employees can be pampered on their days off. I commend your efforts. I have a few more questions, which I'll email to you. In general, I approve of everything you've done. I'd like you to display the model in the main lobby to show everyone what the future holds. I believe the display will be nothing short of inspiring."

"Thank you, sir. I'll relay those thoughts to the team."

"You do that."

Ortiz left Benjamin's office obviously pleased with himself. Benjamin's phone alerted him that he had an urgent call. The caller was Carl Haynes. What was so important that Carl was calling? He put the phone to his ear.

"Hello, Carl. Always a pleasure to hear from you."

"I'm in the lobby, Benjamin. Tell security to let me up. Apparently, it doesn't matter to them that I'm still your boss. No one can see you without an appointment, and I'm not on today's list."

Fifteen minutes later, Carl Haynes sat comfortably in a cozy corner of Benjamin's massive top floor office. Benjamin set a bottle of sparkling water and a glass with a small plate of lemon peels on the brass coffee table separating them. He settled into his white leather chair, wondering what in hell had precipitated Carl's visit.

"If you came for the phase two dog and pony show, you just missed it, but we can review the model together, if you like. I'm still all tingles from the presentation."

He waited as Haynes took a slug of his water. "Or is this a surprise inspection?"

"This is no laughing matter. I came in person to avoid the possibility of any part of our conversation being recorded."

Benjamin felt a jolt of adrenaline race through his body. He braced for the worst while remaining outwardly calm.

"We have a situation at the Mars base," Carl began. "I received a report from the audit team leader, Logan Marchant. One of your robots refused to allow someone named Rashawn Livingston access to a doorway in the mine during a routine structural inspection."

Benjamin almost heaved a sigh of relief. "Where exactly did this happen?"

"Near the drilling rig at the rock face."

"There's a very good reason for that. I'm surprised our Operations Manager didn't explain the situation directly to Commander Marchant."

"The Operations Manager referred the incident all the way up the line to me."

"Well, it hardly sounds like an incident, Carl."

"It became an incident when your robot grabbed this Livingston guy after he insisted on being allowed into the room."

"In the first place, we only open that door when it becomes absolutely necessary because the drill bits are stored there inside a temperature-controlled room. The airlock is state-of-the-art, but we still lose some atmosphere every time someone enters the room. The robots are programmed to only allow authorized personnel into the room when given a coded command by the Operations Manager. The code changes per occurrence for security reasons. We can't have people opening that door any time they please because we can't have the atmosphere compromised. The drill bits can rust easily if we don't maintain the proper temperature and humidity. As to the second part of the so-called incident, can you tell me exactly how the robot 'grabbed' Livingston?"

"He grabbed him by the wrist."

"Did the robot encircle Livingston's wrist with its fingers or did he pull him in some way?"

"This isn't a goddamned courtroom, Benjamin. The robot put hands on Livingston. The man felt threatened. That's a problem. Are the robots allowed to manhandle people?"

"I'm not sure if the robots are programmed to 'put hands,' as you say, on the human mining staff if they do something out of line. I'll have to inquire into the situation myself. It sounds to me like the whole thing got blown out of proportion. But I'll certainly make sure that something like this never happens again."

"Make sure the damn situation gets smoothed out. The last thing we need to do is ruffle the feathers of the pain-in-the-ass audit team."

"I'm right with you there."

"Have you made any progress with the equipment issue?"

"We're still experiencing a high incidence of glitches with the machinery at both of the mining sites. We haven't been able to find a pattern in the breakdowns, which suggests the Martian atmosphere is the culprit. I've spoken to Kaminsky about the situation and we've decided to initiate a program of daily maintenance. We'll be consuming more spare parts and reducing our output slightly. It's the best practice we can come up with until the engineers can zero in on what's causing the problem."

"We're getting reports of reactor malfunctions from a few cities here and abroad." Carl said. "The scientists are working on improving the reactor design. I'm sure they'll figure it out."

Benjamin said nothing in response to the news about the reactors. They spent the next half-hour discussing the business model and profit projections. Benjamin succeeded in buoying Carl's spirits, as usual. Haynes left with a firm handshake and some encouraging words, which Benjamin didn't need. The mining project was going well. In fact, the results thus far had been much better than expected.

He stared out of the floor-to-ceiling, hurricane-proof windows of his penthouse office. There was nothing like a South Florida pink and purple sunset to restore one's faith in nature. That faith needed a lot of restoring these days. The building code required all high-rise structures in Miami-Dade County to have two-hundred-and- fifty per mile per hour wind-resistant windows installed. Killer storms ravaged the east coast from Maine to the Florida Keys with increasing regularity. The MMI building had been hit twice already with minimal damage thanks to its superior construction.

The world desperately needed clean energy to restore its biosphere. He had badly wanted to be the man chiefly responsible for reversing the destructive effects of global warming. If only he had known what he knew now. But then, who could have dreamed he would wind up in this position? Whatever happened, he knew one thing: Benjamin Caliphas would stay in front of the situation and come out on top.

# Chapter 9

# MARS—ARABIA TERRA PLAINS

DMITRI SEMEROV STEERED the rover in the direction of the signal. He and his mission mate, Jon "Hollywood" Henderson, could hardly believe their ears.

"It has to be a false signal," Henderson commented dryly.

"Either that, or we're dreaming,"

Henderson didn't laugh at the remark. Dmitri didn't blame him. He didn't know what to make of the situation. Neither of them did. Jon's banter usually filled the gaps in their conversations when they had their video log turned off. His uncharacteristic silence made the situation more unnerving.

"Turning to check out a signal," Dmitri reported to base.

As they followed the new course, the signal grew louder. Henderson glanced at the digital readout from the anemometer mounted on the rover's roof.

"Wind speed is only two knots. Damn. It can't be a ghost signal. There's hardly a breath of wind out there."

In fact, the weather was about as benign as Dmitri had seen it on the frozen desert world he and Jon now called home. The sun glinted off the reddish-brown sand and rocks on the flat plain in front of them. With no discernable obstacles in their way, they expected to reach their destination soon.

The rover dipped into a depression. The ice formations at the bottom of the crevice spoke to Dmitri of the coming winter. The winter ice formations in the Arabia Terra region brought life-giving water and a welcome respite from these fruitless prospecting missions. The rover carried a specialized Geiger counter calibrated to detect subtle Micromium emissions. To date, their sensors had registered only a few false signals eventually attributed to reflected radio waves from the Communications Array, or high winds. Today's mission brought them too far from base to be picking up man-made signals bounced off rocks or crater walls.

The rover crested the other side of the depression. About five hundred meters ahead, sunlight defined the wall of a crater. According to his calculations, the signal originated from somewhere inside the crater.

"Turn on the camera and watch what you say."

"You don't have to tell me that every time," Henderson complained.

"Yes, I do. Your genius for inappropriate remarks never ceases to embarrass and amaze me."

"You'd be bored stiff on these missions without my gift for scintillating conversation."

He hated to admit Henderson's humor at times kept him from falling asleep at the wheel. At last, some excitement. *Be grateful,* he told himself. Dmitri consulted the digital map of the terrain displayed on the dashboard.

"We're approaching an uncharted crater about forty-five hundred meters due west of base. The signal is increasing in strength. Are you getting this, base?"

\* \* \*

"Monitoring your progress," Oscar Kaminsky answered from his horribly open office in the Operations Array. Before the arrival of the audit team, he had rarely found it necessary to shield himself from his co-workers. Now he needed a bank vault.

Oscar made his reply sound routine. Dmitri would be wondering if the Body Snatchers had stolen his body and made him a pod person. Alone in his excuse-for-a-living-space, he had watched the third remake of the classic horror film last night. Scary movies and jacking off were basically his only forms of recreation. Such were the sacrifices necessary for acquiring the great wealth promised to him in a few short years.

Truth be told, he wanted to jump up and shout "Hallelujah" at the top of his lungs. He just couldn't do it with Commander Marchant and his bitchy sidekick, Kate Blackstone, sitting across from him like two fifteenth century Grand Inquisitors.

"Is everything all right?" Logan asked.

"The rover got stuck in a crevice. The guys have it under control. It happens a lot. My men know what to do."

"Should we table this conversation for later?"

Kaminsky fingered his left earbud for effect. "They're on the move again. Problem solved." He watched Marchant resume a comfortable position in his seat.

"It's interesting that you can carry on two conversations at once with your earbuds on," Kate said.

"Yeah, these two-way buds are pretty amazing." He pulled off one of the buds. "You see this line of tiny holes on the ear frame? It lets me hear conversations in the room. Everybody has to multi-task here; especially now, since we're down two people." Kaminsky paused, as if to observe a moment of silence for the two fallen miners. "You were saying, Corporal Blackstone?"

"I've done sonar studies from the surface rim of the crater. The studies indicate the secondary ore deposit in the strip mine is thin. It appears to be shaped like a blanket rather than a vein with depth. The shape suggests that the deposit is the result of a meteor impact, but my topological studies don't back this up. From the evidence I've gathered, the Siloe Patera crater is most likely the result of volcanic activity—in this case, what we call a super-volcano. The eruptions must have had a significant impact on the planet's ecosphere and atmosphere. If I'm correct in my assumption about the origins of the crater, there should be deeper layers of ore underneath the one near the surface. Have you found any?"

"As you folks know, MMI has taken the position that we're not here to determine the origins of the crater. Our studies indicate the existence of deeper layers, but we can only mine one layer at a time. We can't predict with high confidence how much ore the deeper layers will yield. We'll only know when we get there. We've taken substantial quantities of ore from the other vein in the north wall mine. We expect to stay busy at the north wall for years to come. Two major corporations have spent a significant amount of resources on this project. We didn't come all this way to leave empty-handed, but this is a risky business.

"There are a few things you need to keep in mind. The deposits are random events. The ore may turn out to be rare and hard to find. We hope not. What's most important is the two deposits *we have discovered* have already yielded enough ore to satisfy the Earth's energy needs for *at least* the next thirty years, according to our calculations."

Kate leaned forward. Her eyes shined into his. "We came here to get reasonable estimates of the yield."

"I don't have a crystal ball, Corporal, and we can't continue to suspend our mining operations every time you make a study. We're under a great deal of pressure to keep the ore supply moving. You'll have to do whatever it is you feel you need to do without disturbing our operations and without putting yourselves in harm's way."

"This is not the kind of cooperation we expected," Logan said. "I have to remind you that there is a court order—"

"I've read the court order thoroughly. It compels us to provide you and your team with whatever information you request, but it clearly doesn't require us to shut down our business operations to comply with those requests. I've discussed this matter with my supervisor, Mr. Benjamin Caliphas, who happens to be the CEO of MMI, and he fully supports my position."

"Which means we can't fully discharge the duties we've been assigned by the WEC."

Kaminsky threw up his hands. "We are simply trying to discharge *our* duties, Commander."

"You refused my Flight Engineer's request to access a storage area in the mine."

"And you received a response from a Courtland top executive explaining why that request was refused."

"I hope you can do better than the boiler plate explanation Carl Haynes offered."

"The robots are capable of intelligent thought. Their AI is highly advanced. This one reacted to a situation we've never had before. Our people don't go where they aren't allowed, especially after a proper warning from a human *or* a robot. The robot reacted the way it did. No one was hurt. Live and learn. We've adjusted the programming to make sure no robot will ever lay a hand on your people again. Are you satisfied now?"

"No. I'll notify the WEC oversight committee of your reluctance to allow us full access to make on site ore studies. We'll see what they say. We're done for now. Let's go, Kate."

Kaminsky watched them leave the area while exchanging some undoubtedly choice remarks. *Hell, there's enough Micromium here to make everyone back on Earth happy, if the seas don't down us first.*

"What's going on?" he asked Dmitri.

"We're going behind the crater where our scan shows there's an opening in the wall. Hold on a minute."

Kaminsky worked on a yield report while he awaited further word from his men. Finding another ore site would come in handy right about now. *Oh boy, would it ever.*

The connection crackled with atmospheric interference. Then he heard Dmitri say, "Holy shit, Chief. You won't fucking believe this."

# Chapter 10

# MARS—UNCHARTED CRATER

DMITRI THOUGHT THE body of the giant ship bore a striking resemblance to a streamlined lizard. Boomerang wings studded with massive engines extended from the rear of the fuselage. The size of the craft dwarfed the rover. Awestruck, he observed the vessel. He noticed it rested on a cylindrical support underneath its belly and had claw-like supports under the cockpit and front wings.

"We found a spacecraft in the crater," Dmitri reported back to base. The calm tone of his voice surprised him.

"Another crashed ship?" Kaminsky's voice betrayed an odd mixture of disbelief, anxiety, and excitement.

"No, Oscar. This baby is a hundred percent in one piece and in ever-loving living color. I'm going to drive around it to give you a good look. Turn on your video feed."

Dmitri felt his body tense as they began to move around the ship. Would somebody or something come out to greet them—or maybe kill them?

"Is this ship some sort of secret NASA or WEC mission they forgot to tell us about?" Henderson wanted to know.

"If it was and I knew about it, I'm sure I couldn't tell you,"

Kaminsky replied. "Let me just tell you straight, Hollywood. "What we're looking at ain't no secret mission."

"Then what is it?"

"If it's what I think it is, then it's none of your business."

"Gee, thanks."

As they continued their surveillance, Dmitri pointed at the ship's hull. "You see how the color changes from a leaden gray to a brilliant silver. It almost looks like the ship is breathing."

"Or maybe trying to wake up," Henderson put in.

"Or maybe hibernating," Kaminsky said.

Dmitri steered the rover underneath the ship's right wing. Peering upward, he noticed symbols: a large circle with a smaller, fiery circle and an even smaller circle on either side.

"You see that, Oscar? It looks like a planet surrounded by two suns and two moons."

"I need more light to see it clearly," Kaminsky replied.

"You want us to do an EVA to get more light on it?" Henderson asked.

They waited for Kaminsky to decide. "Yes," came the reply after about thirty tense seconds.

After depressurization, Henderson left the rover armed with a hand-held spot light. He pointed it at the symbols and writing underneath the wing.

The rhythmic color changes of the ship's hull ceased the moment Henderson's light hit the wing.

"It looks like we triggered something," Dmitri reported from inside the rover. "Can you make out the markings now, Oscar?"

"Yeah. I can't hold my water any longer. I'm going to the little boy's room. Give me five minutes."

Dmitri turned off the voice recorder. "Okay, Oscar. The sound is off. Go on."

"Henderson, turn off your comm link."

"C'mon, Oscar. I'm a big boy. I can keep a secret."

"This is not for your ears. Switch off."

"I'm out here with my balls on the line and you won't let me in on this? It's undemocratic."

"Stop whining." Kaminsky waited for Henderson to switch off. "I suppose there's no reason to keep this from you, Dmitri. The markings on that ship match the ones we found on the remains of the three half-buried ships at the bottom of Siloe."

"Whoa. You think this ship came here looking for the ones that crashed?"

"Could be."

A door opened at the base of the ship's cylindrical belly support. Bright light from inside the cylinder spilled onto the Martian sand.

A disc descended with a shining form standing on it. Dmitri stared at the thing. It lumbered out onto the Martian soil.

Henderson backed away cautiously towards the rover from underneath the wing.

Dmitri heard Henderson reanimate his communications link. "Open the damn door. I want back in."

When Henderson reached the rover, Dmitri let him back in. "Repressurizing." The oxygen pumps hissed life-giving air back into the rover's cockpit. The O2 pumps were one of Dmitri's favorite backup systems. If your suit depressurized, nothing beat a toasty, oxygen rich cabin.

The thing from the ship began to rumble towards the rover. From a distance, it looked to Dmitri like a metallic muscle builder on treads. It had a central shaft resembling a spine connecting seven (he counted them) metallic balls growing gradually in size from the smallest to the largest one at the top. *What the hell is inside those balls? Explosives? Brains?* One thing he knew for sure: the damn machine was big. It had to be more than nine feet tall.

"Does it look dangerous?"

"How the fuck should I know, Oscar?"

"Do you see any weapons?"

"The whole goddamned thing could be a weapon," Henderson groused. "I say we get the hell out of here."

"Hold your positions," Kaminsky barked. "We have to find out what's inside that ship."

"Let's assume the robot wants to talk to us," Dmitri said. His mouth felt dry.

"I'm assuming it wants to blow us to kingdom come," Henderson said.

"Stay positive," Kaminsky yammered.

The robot-tank kept advancing. Dmitri quietly uttered a prayer in Russian as the shiny thing emerged from underneath the wing into the open plain—only about fifty meters away.

"I didn't sign up for aliens," Henderson said.

"I'm going to strangle you if you make it back here alive," Kaminsky fumed.

Whatever it intended to do, the buff metallic creature stopped about five meters away in the long shadow cast by the rover. The orbs along its spine came to life—blinking on and off in rapid succession. Dmitri felt a cold chill. His heart rate spiked. Either the thing had set itself to explode or it was trying to communicate with them.

Dmitri backed the rover away from the threatening machine.

"Goddammit. Stay where you are," he heard Kaminsky say.

The blinking lights blazed on and off like fireworks at a fourth of July show.

Henderson switched his comm link to an internal channel. "Fuck Kaminsky. Let's get out of here."

Frozen by fear and indecision, Dmitri watched the lights slow down.

Then, he recognized a pattern. The robot was flashing an SOS signal.

# Chapter 11

# MARS—SILOE STRIP MINE

LOGAN FOLLOWED KATE down the steps cut into the side of the strip mine. He held on to the metal guard rail while carefully taking each step down. The less-than-Earth gravity made him feel a bit like an eighty-year-old negotiating a flight of stairs in a townhouse.

Kate's rapid decent down the staircase concerned him. In her apparent excitement to reach the crater's floor, he watched her miss a step and almost fall before regaining her balance by re-gripping the guard rail.

Instinct urged him to call out; to tell her to be careful. Their agreement to maintain radio silence prevented him from doing it. Even though WEC officials had assured them they had full authority to be clambering down into the secondary mine site, they had decided upon a stealthy approach to avoid tangling with the robot miners. Logan had decided to stop asking for cooperation from Kaminsky and his crew. It was time to take matters into their own hands.

Their excursion might have been impossible without the banks of lights positioned on each terrace of the strip mine. Logan imagined having to navigate the craggy mine face with only hand-held and helmet lights to guide them. It would have been dangerous, even for the robots.

The sounds of the moving crane and bucket wheel met them as they reached the bottom. MMI had commissioned a miniaturized version of the giant machines that, in years gone by, had ripped the tops off mountains and destroyed millions of acres of forest land before they were outlawed in 2027.

Logan stepped off the last stair into powdery soil. Kate waited for him a few feet away. The faint light revealed her boots, submerged in the soil past the ankles. He had half a mind to scrub the mission.

Kate seemed oblivious to the footing. She pointed to an area of the pit far away from the spot where the robot miners operated the bucket-wheel crane. He counted three robots. Two of them moved rocks and boulders while a third operated the crane. Logan had hatched a simple mission plan. Phase One involved avoiding any interaction with the robots. Kaminsky had been vague about when the robots would be re-programmed for hands-free interaction with his team. They both had the distinct impression that the Operations Chief resented committing precious time and energy to any job the team requested.

Using a familiar signal, Logan clasped his hands above his head to remind Kate of the safety precautions required for this part of the mission. She jumped and clapped like a little girl, sending up dust plumes from the ground. Then she put her hand on her helmet in front of her mouth as if to say, *what have I done?* He interpreted the pantomime as a lampoon of their need to use the buddy system. Logan sensed Kate's excitement about their decision to unilaterally begin collecting data on the mines. He motioned for her to calm down.

They grabbed hands and walked towards the first location Kate had plotted for the initial reading. Logan made sure their path maintained a respectful distance from the edge of the open pit. Logan imagined the two of them holding hands in a canopied forest with the sun peeking through the overhead trees. Leaves fell and turned colors, as if the speckles of sunlight moving through the tree tops had magical power. They reached a circular clearing and...he caught himself in the daydream. *What on Earth (Mars, stupid) am I doing?* He forced his attention back to carefully taking each step forward in tandem with Kate.

They reached a point farthest away from the crane and the robots. Kate unclipped a miniaturized device designed to pick up the signature of benign Micromium sub-atomic particle emissions. To Logan, the device resembled the head of a Cobra with its poison pouches flared before a strike. Kate made a note of the reading in her PDA. She showed Logan the reading on the Micromium meter; seven and two tenths. Logan shrugged. The reading meant nothing to him. He expected Kate's in-depth explanation back at the base. They needed three readings from equidistant points around the pit. The second and third readings would bring them closer to Morris, Montrose and Malcolm; the imaginary names Logan had assigned to the three robot miners engulfed by the gloom in the distance.

They high-stepped side by side to the southwest corner of the rectangular pit. Logan stifled a laugh, thinking how ridiculous their movements looked in their attempts not to raise dust and trip in the powdery footing. Kate bobbled halfway to their destination. Logan held her upright. A few steps later, Kate returned the favor. They reached the second location without arousing interest from the mechanical miners. Kate took another reading. This one read six and nine tenths. From the look on Kate's face, Logan knew that something about the readings perplexed her. He wanted to talk to her about it, but it would have to wait until they returned to base. For all he knew, the meter might not be registering properly. Kate's reaction might be due to any number of possibilities. He suddenly felt humiliated by all this sneaking around. They had every right to be doing what they were doing. And they had every right to be doing it more safely, with at least one *friendly* robot as backup.

To reach the third location, they had to backtrack around the pit to avoid passing directly behind the miners. The extra movement and high-stepping began to take a toll on them. He noticed Kate checking the Micromium meter for additional readings as they picked their way through the powdery under-footing. One of the solar powered lights illuminating the pit flickered out attracting their attention. He felt pressure in his right hand as Kate tripped and fell. She cried out and tumbled into the pit before he could catch her.

Logan knelt close to the edge. In the semi-darkness from the blown light, he could barely discern the faint outline of Kate's space suit. "Are you okay?" he called down to her. It looked like she had fallen ten meters to the bottom. Kate lay there; mute and motionless. He called her name again. No response. He felt helpless. Jumping down after her would accomplish nothing. He waved his arms over his head at the mechanical miners. One of them looked up and dropped the rock it was holding. It seemed to be able to size up the situation. The next thing he knew, the robot hopped into the pit. In the gloaming light at the bottom, Logan watched the miner scamper over to Kate using its hands and legs, like a Gorilla, to propel itself quickly along the ground.

He watched the miner pick up Kate's lax body. It looked up at him briefly before turning towards the opposite end of the mine. He followed their progress until they disappeared into the shadows. In his haste and worry about Kate's condition, he slipped and fell twice on his way to the opposite side of the strip mine. On the second fall, a warning light on the HUD inside the plastic face of his helmet alerted him to an oxygen leak somewhere in his suit. *Great timing,* he thought. The pressure in his suit held steady for the moment. The leak wasn't a significant breach. Kate's condition remained priority one.

Shadows consumed the far side of the pit due to a gap in the lighting. More lights must have gone out, Logan figured. The robots probably changed the solar batteries for all the lights at the same time. If a few went out prematurely, it wasn't a big deal, because humans rarely visited the mine and the robots had eyes designed to see in the darkness.

As he neared the corner of the mine where the big shovel had been digging, the robot scaled the side of the pit carrying Kate. In the irregular lighting, it looked like the robot walked on air. As he came nearer, Logan saw a straight line of ringed steps jutting from the side of the pit. The robot crested the top of the pit at the same time he arrived.

He noticed Kate's faceplate fog and clear, indicating regular breathing. She was alive. At least she hadn't broken her neck.

"Take her to the lift," he told the robot.

It stood there with Kate in its arms.

"We need to get to the lift. She needs medical assistance."

The robot remained motionless. Evidently, it was not programmed to take orders from him.

Logan radioed the base for help. Kaminsky answered in a tinny voice, probably the result of their distance from the surface.

"What are you doing out there, Marchant? You're supposed to notify us of your activities outside the base."

"I don't have time to explain. Kate's seriously injured and my suit has a leak. Tell your robot to help us get to the surface. And tell the damn thing to take commands from me."

"I'm going to report your reckless behavior."

"Knock yourself out. Just help us to get top side."

Kaminsky did as he was told without further argument. Logan, Kate, and the robot set out for the lift.

By the time they reached the elevator, Logan had lost twenty-five percent of his oxygen supply. Worse still, his suit pressure had dropped fifteen percent. When Kate stirred in the robot's arms, he forgot about his plight immediately. She complained of pain in her right knee and one hellacious headache, but she refused to be carried. When she tried to stand, Logan had to support her with one arm around the waist.

"I feel nauseous," she said.

"You probably have a concussion."

"I'll be okay. I don't think I broke anything, except maybe my skull. Are you okay?"

"I'm fine. Take a few deep breaths. You'd be better off sitting, but I don't want to put you down on this freezing walkway."

The robot pressed the call button for the lift. It would take fifteen minutes to reach them from the surface. Logan had asked Kaminsky to have the lift waiting for them when they arrived. He had explained the elevator could not be activated remotely. He'd probably have enough oxygen to reach the surface where a couple of rovers would meet them with Kaneko waiting in one of them with medical supplies. There was only one problem: the elevator would deliver him frozen to death if his suit pressure kept dropping at its current rate. His fingers and toes already felt numb.

He ordered the robot to prop Kate upright while he ran a full scan to find the leak. The subtle leak stubbornly refused to show up on his suit's auto-detect system.

"Can you detect a space suit leak?" he asked the robot in desperation.

"I will try," it said.

How odd that Kaminsky had not thought to ask the robot to detect the leak. Maybe he didn't know his robots had this capability? Or maybe he did.

"You have a suit leak?" A suit leak is not doing fine, Logan."

"It's just a little one."

Logan grabbed the patching kit from his tool belt, ready to patch away if the robot got lucky.

The robot ran its hands methodically up and down Logan's right leg. It stopped at a point on his shin. "I sense the leak here," it said, applying pressure with two fingers.

Logan applied the patch. *Please God, work*. Kate surprised him when she took his hand. *It's got to work. She likes me*.

A few minutes passed. His suit pressure rose. Feeling slowly returned to his hands and feet.

"How's your oxygen level?"

"Should have enough to reach the rover."

"We keep a supply of oxygen tanks for emergencies in a locker on the lift," the robot announced. "I can hook one up for you."

"That's a good lad. Please oxygenate me."

"I do not understand the command."

"Logan. Be serious."

He rephrased the command in literal terms, feeling deeply grateful and slightly giddy about his chances of seeing the surface again. *And she likes me,* the little boy in him thought. *There is nothing seriously wrong with her,* the man in him affirmed. *I'm waiting,* the deep-down darkness in him grumbled.

Ten minutes later, the lift arrived. The cage door rose vertically and they entered. With a mighty gnashing of gears, they began their ascent to the surface.

Chapter 12

# MARS—ALIEN SHIP

THE HUGE ROBOT motioned to them with arms that looked powerful enough to lift the rover.

"I think it's inviting us into the ship." Dmitri said

"I'm not following that thing anywhere," Henderson said.

"You can get out now and wait for me."

Henderson made no move to leave the rover.

Dmitri put the rover in gear and steered towards the cylindrical support underneath the belly of the ship. Oddly, he felt no fear or the slightest trepidation. Curiosity overwhelmed him. He wanted to see the inside of the ship in the worst way. Since early childhood, Dmitri had developed an intense interest in alien life forms and alien technology. It was the driving force that had propelled him into the space program and extraterrestrial exploration.

The floor of the crater seemed unusually smooth until Dmitri realized the robot was clearing a path for them as they followed it to the ship. Rocks and debris scattered on either side of the robot's tracks as it lumbered along like a snow plow, making their way to the ship straight and safe.

"You see how it's rolling out the red carpet for us, Hollywood. The folks inside that ship must be friendly."

"Maybe they aren't folks. Maybe they're machines like this big mother in front of us. If they *are* living things, maybe they ran out of food and want to eat us for breakfast"

"I love your spirit of adventure. This is your last chance to get out and freeze your ass off. Your chances are fifty-fifty that Oscar will send another rover for you. He's not your biggest fan."

"Very fucking funny."

The robot stopped in front of the cylinder. The ship's central strut was much larger than it appeared from a distance; probably wide enough to transport the rover inside. Dmitri had no intention of going up in the rover, however. Best to leave the rover outside in case they had to leave in a hurry. He didn't want to think about what the atmosphere in the ship might do to their suits.

An oval door opened in the cylinder. Light from inside poured out onto the Martian surface in a spectrum of bright colors. The robot motioned to them again; this time to enter the ship. Dmitri reckoned the colored lights might be a cleansing system to prevent viruses, bacteria, soil, or any contaminating matter to enter the ship. It would not be good manners to drive the rover in; another reason to enter in space suits only, even though it would leave them more vulnerable to the atmosphere inside.

"Permission to enter the ship, Oscar?"

"Permission granted."

"You heard the man. Let's go, Hollywood."

"Shouldn't we leave someone in the rover—just in case?"

Dmitri could almost hear Kaminsky thinking it over. "That's not a bad idea, Hollywood. You stay in the rover. You aren't exactly what I'd call a Good Will Ambassador."

Dmitri shook Henderson's hand. "See you when I see you."

"I doubt I'll be that lucky. Don't do anything stupid and watch your oxygen levels. Keep your comm open."

"Will do."

Dmitri departed the rover. The robot rolled on ahead of him. He watched it disappear into the multi-colored lights. He drew in a deep breath and followed. With the colors rioting around him, he had no sense of the space surrounding him. Somehow, it didn't bother him. A peaceful feeling stole over him. He sensed the lights doing something to his suit and to him. He felt taken care of; an unexpected sense of relief, and a subtle movement upwards. It seemed like an energy field generated by the disc underneath him was gently transporting him into the ship. He closed his eyes and soon drifted off into a dreamless sleep.

He awoke lying on a white table. When he sat up, Dmitri felt the surface of the table shift to conform to his movements. The table felt like a fleshy palm that supported him comfortably. He felt energized and a bit light-headed. He looked down to check his oxygen meter. He saw only his bare arm. Someone had removed his spacesuit; yet he had no difficulty breathing. He felt vulnerable wearing only his thermal underwear. Without his comm link, he worried about losing contact with Kaminsky and Henderson.

Eight pods surrounded him. Darkness lurked beyond the pods. Considering the ship's long fuselage, he knew the interior had to be much larger than the visible space around him. He had the impression that the ship's occupants or its computer had deliberately kept his field of vision limited to the relatively small circle of pods. It occurred to him that the pods were individual life support systems. As he thought this, a faint light glimmered from inside the pod to his immediate right. *It's trying to awaken,* he thought. And then he had the oddest impression that the thought came from somewhere other than his own mind.

The robot appeared suddenly from out of the darkness, startling him. It looked like the same robot that had greeted them outside, except now it had a set of gracefully fashioned metal and translucent plastic arms instead of the heavy lifters it wore outside. With an elegant plastic forefinger, it pointed to the glimmering pod. The black outer shell of the pod changed gradually into a perfectly transparent outer covering. Inside, yellow, green and gold gases swirled around a woman's face. He knew it was a woman's face; yet she looked like no other woman he had ever laid eyes upon.

Her head and shoulders appeared three times larger than human size. Her sunken cheeks and white skin belied the slow rise and fall of her chest. Life stirred in that body. Oh, what a beautiful body! Her features appeared sculpted from stone by an Italian Maestro. Trellises of russet hair framed the face. The hair had grown too long, in waves down her shoulders and along the side of the pod. She wore no clothing. The gasses obscured parts of her lower body. What he saw looked human in every detail—and powerfully alluring. Dmitri seriously considered that all of this was a dream. Soon, he would wake up in his pitiful bunk bed back at the base, bitterly disappointed.

"Why are they asleep?" Dmitri decided to ask the robot, hoping it could understand the question.

"*There has been a malfunction,*" the robot answered telepathically.

"How do you know my language?"

"*The ship has scanned your mind and learned how to speak with you.*"

"What else has the ship learned from scanning my mind?"

"*The ship has not shared that information with me.*"

"Did you ask me aboard to pick my brain?"

The robot extended its powerful right arm and opened its palm: "*No. We need your help. Several of the ship's systems sustained damage during the voyage here, including the reawakening function of the stasis pods. The ship is like an organism. One system malfunction can set off additional malfunctions. The three backup systems for the pods have failed. The mathematical chances of this happening are four hundred and thirty six thousand, three hundred and eighty-two to one. I am not designed to deal with this situation, and the ship cannot fix the problem by itself. It needs help. Will you ask your software engineers to come here to resolve the problem?*"

"What makes you think our engineers can help?"

"*I don't know if they can help, but it is worth trying. The ship and your engineers can work together. We must awaken the crew.*"

"I'd like to know why you came here. I assume you came from far away."

"*Our primary mission is to see if this planet is suitable for colonization. Our world is over-populated. Our two suns are dying. This is one of the planets we identified that can be made habitable with terraforming. We have brought the terraforming equipment with us.*"

Dmitri labored to remain calm while processing the robot's surprising answer to his question. "We have two colonies here already. Eventually, we plan to establish many more. There is a big chance your goals will conflict with ours.

"*If we terraform the planet, we will make life here more desirable for your future colonists. We come here in friendship. We have no desire to compete with you. We expect there will be cooperation and collaboration between our races. We have much to offer. Our world has many similarities to your home world. Our atmosphere is almost identical to yours. We have evolved in much the same way as your species, except for the difference in the size of our bodies. Our home planet is five times the size of yours.*"

"You seem to know a lot about us."

"*We studied your world, this planet, and your entire solar system with an undetectable deep-space probe. The probe has long since stopped sending us information. Because of the distance between our worlds, the information about a civilization like yours becomes quickly dated. I am sure you can understand this. Your space program, for instance, has progressed far beyond the sub-orbital and orbital flights we monitored before our probe stopped transmitting.*"

"You said your primary reason for coming here is colonization. Is there another reason?"

"*Three of our ships came here before us. Those ships crashed for no apparent reason. We came here to find out why the ships crashed.*

*So, they did come here looking for their ships*, Dmitri said to himself. *Oscar's going to shit a brick.*

"This ship seems very big for a crew of eight."

The robot pointed upwards. Soft lighting suddenly illuminated an extremely high ceiling. "*This ship can carry up to twenty-four hundred citizens, plus a crew of twenty. The extra living quarters have been removed to reduce the strain on the ship's resources. The only remaining living quarters are situated behind the balconies lining both walls near the ceiling. When they awaken, the crew will enjoy suites of spacious apartments, gyms, recreation rooms, and offices. We are an expeditionary force. Our mission will take several orbits around your sun. The ship is designed for our comfort and safety while we are here."*

Dmitri suddenly felt a heavy mantle of responsibility descend upon his shoulders. The aliens might have a great deal to offer the people of Earth. Could we trust them? Could they trust us?

"Before I leave, I'd very much like to see the rest of your ship."

The robot cocked its head, as if considering Dmitri's request.

*"There will be time for that. The priority is to reanimate the crew. They cannot remain in stasis much longer without harm to their vital organs. Will you help us?"*

Dmitri's heart sank. He desperately wanted to see more of the ship.

"I'll talk to my superiors. Where is my spacesuit?"

*"I will bring it."* Turning deftly, the robot wheeled away.

# Chapter 13

# MARS—MEDICAL BAY

LOGAN KNOCKED ON the open med bay door.

"Yeah?" came the response from behind the curtains surrounding Kate's bed.

"It's Logan. May I come in?"

"It's about time you showed up."

He took that as a "yes."

"Sorry for the delayed visit, but Kaneko wouldn't let me come near you until today."

Logan approached the bed at the same time Kate pulled open the curtains. Despite the wrinkled hospital gown and no makeup, she looked damned good for someone who had taken a thirty-foot fall and suffered a serious concussion.

"Hand me the mirror and brush on the dresser and give me a minute to look human."

Kate stroked the tangles out of her hair and laid the brush and mirror down.

"Besides righteously pissed off, how do you feel?"

"If they don't let me out of here soon, I'll give myself another concussion from banging my head against the walls."

"Kaneko said you'll be released soon. The observation period is almost over and you've been acing all of your tests."

Kate waived off his attempt to buoy her spirits. "Logan, the readings we took from the strip mine are lower than I expected. I'd say the deposit will be depleted in five years or less at the rate they're taking the ore out of the ground. I'll make a more accurate estimate once I'm allowed to get back to work."

"We're not going back down there any time soon," Logan said dryly.

"We don't have to. I have enough data from my readings to do the calculations. I just need to know the capacity and speed of the bucket shovel they're using."

"I really wish you'd concentrate on healing rather than working. Your brain got smacked pretty hard."

"I've been cooperating fully with Kaneko's treatment program. I don't need a lot of brain cells to predict the remaining life span of that deposit."

Logan heard a light knock from behind.

"Come in, Kaneko. You aren't interrupting anything important. Logan is just doing his 'let's make Kate feel better' thing."

Kaneko entered the room with a sweet smile, clutching a medical tablet to her breast. She ran a hand through her straight black hair. Her brown oval eyes reflected both intensity and calm. The room seemed to brighten with her presence.

"Logan is sincerely concerned about you, dear Kate. You're fortunate to have such a caring commanding officer."

Logan felt himself blush. Sometimes he wished Kaneko wasn't as honest in speaking her feelings and observations.

Logan stood by while Kaneko checked Kate's eye movements with a mini- flashlight. Then she asked Kate to follow her finger movements with her eyes. Finally, she nodded.

"Your eye movements are back to normal, Kate. I'm going to release you, but I'm placing some restrictions on what you can and cannot do. We've only had you here for a week. Your brain will take several months to heal completely. From the scan we took yesterday, I don't see any evidence of scarring or signs of lasting damage. Your helmet cushioned enough of the blow to prevent complications. You may experience headaches and dizzy spells in the next few weeks, but those symptoms should disappear if you follow my directions. With your consent, I'll give Commander Marchant a full report of your condition and my recommendations."

"What if I don't give my consent?"

"Then I'll keep you here indefinitely."

"I hate you, Kaneko."

Kaneko responded with a faint smile.

Kate smiled back. "I appreciate everything you've done for me. You're a brilliant healer and I'm a terrible patient."

"Yes, you are, but you did your part and I expect you to keep doing it. I'll file the paperwork and then we'll meet in my office in about an hour to talk about where we go from here. Bye for now."

Kaneko smiled and waved to Kate and Logan and then they were alone again.

Kate propped herself up in bed. "Can you tell me what's been going on while I've been cooped up in this lovely hotel?"

"You really should be grateful that you can expect a full recovery."

"I am. Speak."

Logan pulled up a chair next to the bed. He swung a leg over the top and sat.

"I made my report to the WEC oversight committee about the lack of cooperation we're getting from the mining staff. They assured me steps will be taken to improve the situation. Reading between the lines, I think the committee won't support us as much as we'd like them to. It's a political situation. The committee is more interested in the uninterrupted flow of ore than in what we're doing. We're kind of on our own. The most prudent way to proceed, I think, is to do our investigation as best we can and get off this rock with as much information as we can gather. I'm not going to risk the lives of my crew. I've been disciplined for our secret mission to the strip mine. I'm responsible for your accident."

"It wasn't your fault."

"It was a bad decision on my part."

Kate inhaled deeply. "I suppose we'll have to be good boys and girls and do everything by the book from now on."

"It looks that way."

They sat there staring into one another's eyes for only a few seconds before he had to look away. "There's something else. I really shouldn't be telling you this. Please keep it confidential."

She nodded.

"Kaminsky and two of his mining supervisors have been acting strangely. They went to the Communications Array yesterday. I asked Kaminsky if everything was all right. He told me they're doing routine maintenance to the equipment out there. The outpost is about a mile from the base. I don't know much about the equipment, but it doesn't make sense that Kaminsky would assign three men, including himself, to a routine maintenance job. Something unusual is going on out there."

"We've had the feeling they haven't been up front with us from the beginning."

"This is different. I can't put my finger on it, but I know it's not the same smoke screen we've been getting. I mean, now it feels like there's something significant going on underneath the surface. Whatever it is, they clearly don't want us to know anything about it. It could be dangerous for us to find out what they're up to."

"Whatever's going on, we have to get out to the north wall mine site to do some tests."

"I'm not sure 'we' includes you, at this point. It depends on what Kaneko recommends for your activities going forward."

"Don't give me the 'going forward' bullshit, Logan. I'm the only one who can do those tests."

"Do I have to remind you that I'm your CO?"

Splaying ten fingers on her forehead, Kate looked down at the bed. "Sorry. I didn't mean any disrespect." Shaking her head, she looked up at him. "This is all so frustrating."

"We can't let them know we suspect anything."

"I hear you."

He took her hand. He couldn't help it. His hand had a mind of its own. She compressed her hand in his. What were they doing holding hands? He felt the maw of the pit in his guts open, beckoning him to drop in for a nightmarish visit. She made him feel too deeply. It hurt.

"Let's see what Kaneko has to say."

She withdrew her hand from his and held it protectively, as if it were guilty of some crime. She looked up at him and nodded.

He picked himself up from the chair. He wanted to wrap his fucking arms around her and hold her. He wanted to kiss her. He wanted to rip her pajamas off and...*enough*. He shut the door on these thoughts. They could scuttle his career as a deep space astronaut if he allowed them into the light. They could drag him down into the pit and drown him.

He wheeled out of the med bay, boiling with conflicting emotions.

* * *

In the Communications Array, the three men waited for Benjamin Caliphas to respond. Thanks to advanced laser and broadband technology, the time lapse for communications between Earth and Mars had been reduced to a little less than five minutes. Radio wave communication had been phased out in favor of binary electronic messages riding on high-intensity laser beams.

Despite the improved communications lag, company policy prohibited Kaminsky and his men from discussing MMI business over an open channel. MMI allowed its employees to chat live with their spouses and families, but these conversations were closely monitored, and any mention of company business was strictly forbidden.

In most cases, the mining staff transmitted company business to MMI headquarters in encrypted data bits via secure channels. Only dire emergencies or highly unusual circumstances permitted live interplanetary conversations about company business. Oscar Kaminsky, Dmitri Semerov and Jon Henderson huddled in front of a communications console, smack in the middle of highly unusual circumstances. They stared up at a ten by ten-foot screen, waiting for the next burst of electrons to animate the motionless face of Benjamin Caliphas towering above them.

In the silence, Oscar observed the facial features of his boss. He rarely came face to face with his boss. The suspended animation effect gave Oscar a rare opportunity to observe his features. Caliphas owned the full lips of a lover, but the way he held them in a contracted position betrayed a hint of cruelty. His eyes sparkled with intelligence and a certain quality Oscar perceived as wildness. Raven black hair and eyebrows lent Caliphas a fierce look. God had blessed Benjamin Caliphas with even features and good looks. He charmed and motivated his people. Oscar gladly did whatever Caliphas asked of him. Now, staring into Benjamin's electronic portrait, caught like an insect fossilized in amber, Oscar felt a cold fear bubbling in his entrails. The red numerals in the center of the console counted down to single digits, indicating a transmission coming in. When the numerals turned green, Caliphas came to life.

"Obviously I'm surprised by this news," Caliphas began. "I'm not going to be careful with what I'm about to say because Oscar has assured me the auto record function is disabled. So, to answer your question: we cannot, until I've had a chance to think this through, help the alien robot reanimate the crew of the ship. The alien ship represents a potential disaster to our entire operation unless I or we can figure out how to make the situation work for us. If you have any suggestions, I'll listen to them now. Over to you."

Caliphas went into hibernation again with his mouth puckered in a kiss from the utterance of his last vowel sound. Not one of them dared to laugh at the lifeless image.

"We've discussed the issue thoroughly," Oscar said. "Dmitri has something to say. Jon and I don't support his point of view, but he wants to be heard. Go ahead, Dmitri."

"It is very difficult to put my experience in the ship into words, Mr. Caliphas. I was filled with a sense of awe and wonder. I can't tell you how or why, but I sensed a magnificence and nobility emanating from the aliens sleeping in the pods. They are exactly like us in every detail, only they are about three times larger in size."

Oscar knew Dmitri had more to say, but he seemed to pause and look inward, considering his words carefully. Oscar braced himself for what might come next. Their discussion here, yesterday, had been heated, but he knew that Dmitri's position needed to be expressed, whatever the consequences.

Dmitri leaned forward with his hands in a conjuring pose.

"It occurred to me while I was a guest aboard the ship that we are as alien to this planet as these visitors are. I know only a little about these people, but I felt a definite kinship with them. I feel strongly that it is our duty to help these people in any way that we can. I'm certain these people mean us no harm. I'm equally certain they have no interest in our business here. The presence of these visitors represents an immeasurable learning opportunity for us and every human being on Earth. These visitors will cooperate peacefully with us. I trust my instincts implicitly on everything I've said. The way forward in this situation is to reanimate, learn from, and work with the visitors. This course of action will benefit us enormously."

Dmitri leaned back in his chair, obviously spent from the emotion of his words. Oscar had to admit that the presentation had inspired him. Some spark in him had been reanimated like the visitors Dmitri wanted to help. Some things went beyond dollars and cents. Dmitri had made a convincing argument that this situation transcended commerce. Would Caliphas buy it?

Ten minutes elapsed. If not for the green light in the bottom left-hand corner of the screen indicating the link with Earth remained intact, Oscar would have guessed Caliphas had hung up on them. His voice finally came through with a slight doppelgänger effect due to some interference, but the meaning of the words came through unmistakably.

"Your points are well made, Dmitri. I applaud your altruism. There certainly is a lot at stake here. Try to understand that I cannot permit anyone to board the ship again until I've had more time to consider the situation. Until you hear further from me, the alien ship does not exist. I am asking the three of you to guard this secret zealously. Are we clear?"

The three men gave Caliphas their assurances and then signed off.

"We don't know how long the visitors can survive in suspended animation if their life support system is compromised." Dmitri said as soon as the big screen turned black.

"It's a big decision," Oscar said. "We can't do anything without Caliphas' approval."

Dmitri slumped in his chair.

Henderson regarded Dmitri balefully. "Orders are orders, pal."

"Be patient," Oscar said. "Caliphas will make the right call."

Dmitri looked back at him with a curious look of wild-eyed intensity. Oscar wondered if something had happened to him aboard the alien ship.

# Chapter 14

# EARTH—MMI HEADQUARTERS

SEATED IN HIS ergonomic black leather chair, Benjamin leaned back from his massive clear plastic and bronze desk. He already had the best of everything, and it was only going to get better. In the years ahead, he expected his companies to earn gargantuan profits from the new products they developed.

In addition to this bounty, Benjamin had a huge problem weighing heavily on his expensive desk and his conscience. He had considered the possibility of another alien expedition following up on the first one. He had no way of calculating the odds of such an event materializing. Now it had happened.

He would deal with this challenge no differently than he had with all the others: boldly and creatively. Every problem had an optimal solution waiting to be discovered. Rather than panic, he thought of the situation as just another problem awaiting a best-case solution.

He dismissed, without a second thought, Dimitri Semorov's idiotic proposal. How could Semerov have the audacity to make such a plea knowing the risks involved? The man had clearly lost his senses. Had the aliens brainwashed him? Whatever the case, Semerov could no longer be trusted.

The computer screen inlaid in Benjamin's desk chirped a reminder about his weekly teleconference with Carl Haley scheduled to begin in five minutes. As the minutes chimed down, a plan formed in Benjamin's fertile mind.

Carl's face populated outward from the center of the screen. For his amusement, Benjamin had set up the video feed to simulate the Big Bang effect of the beginning of the universe when images appeared. Despite a recent facelift, Carl's face looked drawn and haggard.

"You look a bit frayed around the edges, my friend," Benjamin commented.

"It's been a week and a half around here. I could use some good news."

"You could have invited me over for our weekly chat. We're only three buildings apart. You always feel better when you see me in person."

"Three of our divisions lost big contracts. I've been in meetings all week, listening to excuses. The one bright spot in the ointment is the consistency of the ore flow. What else do you have for me?"

"Before I tell you, turn off your recorder and delete the file."

"It's that bad?"

"I wanted to tell you in person. Your secretary told me you've been tied up. I told her not to bother you."

Benjamin waited for Haynes to delete the record of their conversation.

"Okay. We're clear. Shoot."

Benjamin knew that what he was about to say would shake the most grizzled veteran to his or her foundations. He didn't see any other feasible choice.

"Here's the good news. On an ore prospecting mission, we discovered a completely intact alien space ship with a live crew hidden inside an uncharted crater."

"You're serious?"

"Deadly serious. This discovery presents us with a tremendous opportunity. It can also be a complete disaster if we don't handle it properly."

Benjamin gave Haynes a few moments to absorb the shock of his announcement.

"Explain."

"I'm impressed by the way you're taking this, Carl. From the information I've gathered, the ship we found is on a follow-up mission to an initial mission that failed tragically. My men found the wreckage of three alien ships at the bottom of the Siloe Patera Crater during our mining operation. We did not announce this discovery to the world because what we've dredged up from the wreckage will generate trillions of dollars in profits with the products and services that can be developed from the extraordinary alien technology we've excavated. We'll be able to cure deadly diseases and reverse the aging process, for starters. I'm talking about advancements in just about every area of human endeavor."

Benjamin increased the resolution of Carl's manicured face, which sported a handle bar mustache and Van Dyke beard. In the background of the inlaid screen, photos showed a smiling Haynes with his trophy wife on board their fishing boat. They stood next to a huge tarpon and a sailfish dangling from heavy chains. Benjamin eliminated the background photos to concentrate on his subject's facial reactions.

Haynes brought a hand up to his cheek and tilted his head slightly. "The obvious question is: why didn't you bring the wrecked alien ships and the technology to my attention?"

"Frankly, my team and I wanted to keep the profits for ourselves. We've almost completed the drawings and the notes we'll need to recreate the technology back on Earth. We intended to bury the original artifacts in a remote location. I see now that my original plan was sheer folly."

"And now you want to share the profits with MMI and Courtland?"

"Yes. Everyone profits: MMI, Courtland, you, me—everyone walking on the planet."

"This is all very troubling. Your actions, Benjamin, are extremely disturbing. I believed in you. How do you expect me to trust you now?"

"I've given up the deception. I've come clean with you. I've held nothing back. We can work together or go down together. If you tell the Board what I've done, they'll hold you responsible, too. We'll go down in flames and maybe wind up in jail. Tell me what you want to do."

"Let's be honest, Benjamin. The discovery of the live alien ship has complicated your scheme. It's grown too big to cover up. That's why you've come to me with this sudden burst of altruism."

"I didn't want to get into a big hassle over the intellectual property rights. Yes, I should have confided in you. I didn't want to risk news of the discovery leaking out. I know this looks bad, Carl, but my way of dealing with the situation ensures that the benefits of this new technology will reach the masses sooner. And yes, I admit to being greedy."

"Have you communicated with the passengers aboard the ship?"

"They're asleep. Their hyper-sleep system failed to awaken them. A caretaker robot aboard the ship has asked for our help to reanimate the crew. I don't believe it is in our interest to explore this possibility."

"Explain."

"One of my men boarded the ship and talked at length with the robot. Apparently, the second alien expedition came here to determine why the first mission failed and to carry forward their plans to terraform Mars. The robot offered assurances of the visitors' complete cooperation and non-interference with our presence here. The robot implied the alien presence on Mars will serve to enhance our objectives here, presumably with the deployment of an Earth-like atmosphere and by sharing their advanced technology with us."

"In other words, awakening the crew nullifies any claim we could make to the technology."

"Exactly. And we have no idea if the alien crew will keep the robot's promises once they wake up. The robot's claims may be an elaborate deception. For all we know, the aliens intend to use Mars as a staging area to invade the Earth."

Benjamin watched Haynes close his eyes. He could almost read his thoughts. A full minute passed during which Haynes brought his palm to his forehead in deep reflection, then he spoke, as Benjamin hoped he would. He needed Haynes to convince himself of what they must do.

"So, you let the crew die or disable their life support system. Then we announce this remarkable discovery to the world and stake our claim."

"I think it's the only option under the circumstances," Benjamin said. We'll be heroes — incredibly rich heroes."

"There will be a huge battle over who owns the rights to the technology."

"Yes, and while it rages, we'll form a new company and patent products based on the drawings we made from the technology recovered from the three doomed ships. No one will ever know they existed, except you, me, and my staff here. And here's the kicker. I'll offer you a big position in the new company at three times your salary, plus stock options. What do you say?"

"Hmmm. I just got a promotion. Are all of your people on board with this?"

"They've gone along with me this far. They can't turn back. To ensure their loyalty, I'll give them a bigger piece of the pie."

Haynes sighed deeply. "I guess we have no choice. Go ahead with your plan, and make goddamned sure you keep me in the loop this time."

# Chapter 15

# MARS—MEDICAL
# AND EXOBIOLOGY OFFICE

LOGAN THOUGHT KANEKO'S office reflected the multi-dimensional persona of the woman he had come to know and deeply respect. From tiny seed packets, she had cultivated a menagerie of flowering plants from her native Japan and the western regions of the United States. A Zen garden flourished in one corner of the office. A miniature desert garden encased in glass occupied a shelf above and behind her desk. Modernistic sculptures Kaneko had made from multicolored plastic string and tubes resembling muscle fibers adorned shelves artfully placed at varying heights around the room, from close to the floor to just below the ceiling.

Despite the absence of book shelves, Logan knew Kaneko loved to read medical and science fiction thrillers in addition to literature, philosophy, and theology. Books were a luxury no one on the base could afford, given the constraints of available square footage. All texts, including Kaneko's complete medical and exobiological libraries, existed in digital form.

Amidst these calming and tasteful surroundings, Logan sat comfortably with Kate and Kaneko around another of her plastic sculptures —a blue mushroom-shaped table with a flat top.

They talked about Kaneko's artwork and the unusual beauty she had brought to her small office. Logan remarked that the office itself felt like a living work of art. With her hands pressed together beneath her chin, Kaneko accepted the compliment with a bright smile and a slight bow. Then, she assumed a confident posture and spoke in a kind and reassuring tone.

"I've gone over your tests and treatment charts again, Kate. You've made progress. You can resume most of your duties and a moderate exercise program right away. However, your body and brain still need time to heal. We'll keep you inside the base for another two weeks and then re-evaluate your condition."

Kate turned to Logan with a distressed expression and then looked back at Kaneko.

"Kaneko, we're at a critical point in our investigation. I must perform tests at the north face mine site. I can't go into detail as to why, but it can't wait two weeks."

"I can't allow you outside, Kate. You aren't ready for the changes in air pressure and the extreme physical activity, never mind the danger of falling again."

Kate turned back to him, her normally cool blue eyes ablaze with emotion. "Logan?"

He put a hand on her forearm. It was hard to look directly into the passion in her eyes, but he kept his gaze steady.

"We have to follow Kaneko's instructions." He carefully avoided the word *orders* in the same way he noticed Kaneko had avoided using the word *restrict* regarding Kate's movements. To elicit cooperation from a high-spirited woman like Kate, they knew tact usually worked the best.

Kaneko discreetly changed the subject. Placing her medical tablet on the table, she said: "Now that I have you both here, I'd like to show you something."

She called up a series of images and slid them across the tablet screen for Kate and Logan to view. "I've been microscopically examining soil samples from both mine sites. I've catalogued several simple microorganisms indicative of bodies of water that may have existed here eons ago. Then I came across these, just before our meeting. I'm still trying to recover from the shock and come up with a reasonable hypothesis."

"They look like human cells," Kate said.

"I agree," Kaneko replied. "They appear to be human skin cells, except they are about three times the size of normal human cells."

Logan leaned over the table for a closer look. "How can you tell the cells are abnormally large?"

"I've compared them to scrapings of my own cells. The measurements of the cell nuclei from the soil sample are uniformly larger than human cell nuclei. I haven't had time to carbon date them, but they are remarkably well-preserved. If intelligent life once thrived here, it would have existed millions or billions of years ago, according to all of the studies we've done so far."

"That goes along with my observations," Kate said. "My instincts tell me the planet has been virtually dead for eons."

"It's obviously very unusual to find eons-old cells so close to the planet's surface and in such good condition. It may have something to do with the depth of the crater and the frozen ground. I can't be sure. One thing is certain: if these cells represent the remains of an intelligent race, we should be able to find evidence of an ancient civilization somewhere in the crater."

"It brings up another question," Logan said. "If MMI accidentally discovered artifacts from an ancient civilization, why wouldn't they announce it? Kaminsky would say it's not part of the corporation's business, but the discovery of human-like remains on Mars is something that falls into the public domain. I think MMI would have a duty to report it. When you complete the carbon dating, let's meet again. In the meantime, I have to caution you to keep this discussion and your research to yourself."

Some of the color drained from Kaneko's face. "Why can't I question the mining staff about this? I don't understand."

Kaneko picked up the medical tablet and held it against her chest. "Is there danger?"

"I believe so," Logan said. "We have to be careful. Don't trust anyone employed by the corporation. I'm telling you this for your own safety. If something important comes up before we meet again, bring it to my attention—my attention only."

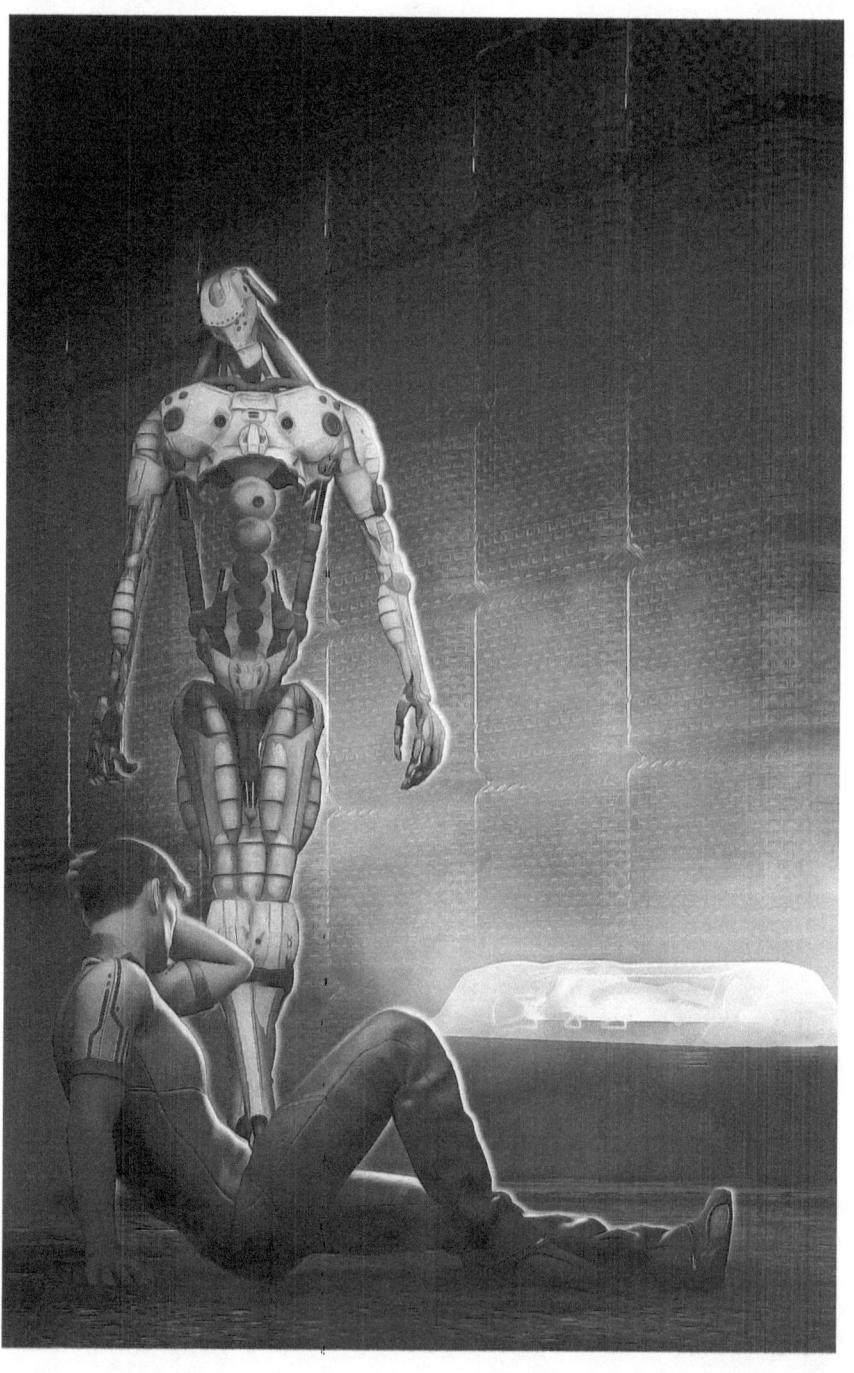

# Chapter 16

# MARS—ROGUE MISSION

THE SUN REFLECTED off the red sand and the hills and valleys comprising the rough landscape of Arabia Terra. With each kilometer of the Martian plain that rolled by outside his rover's window, Dmitri's excitement and anxiety grew. On the plus side, every bumpy meter of the journey brought him closer to the alien ship. On the down side, every turn guided by the memory of the rover's GPS brought him closer to losing everything he had worked for. The source of his courage for this reckless mission mystified him. He had never felt more strongly about anything in his life. Either his humanity had been deeply stirred to action by the situation, or something had happened to him aboard the ship.

Whatever the case, Dmitri had passed the point of no return. He had lied to his superior, Oscar Kaminsky, by logging in false information about the nature of his mission and its destination. By the time Kaminsky figured something was amiss, Dmitri hoped to be aboard the alien vessel.

He carefully avoided the rivulet the rover had slid into on the first trip, he circled the uncharted crater. The sight of the sleek lines and size of the alien craft took Dmitri's breath away, as it had previously, and something else startled him. A blip on his radar screen appeared. Someone had followed him.

He noticed the range between his position and the blip closing steadily. Undoubtedly, Kaminsky had sent someone after him when he diverged from the phony course he had logged. Dmitri was counting on Kaminsky being too busy to notice. It probably meant that he had aroused suspicion after his speech in the Communications Array. So be it. He had plenty to deal with right now—gaining access to the ship.

Exiting the rover, Dmitri strode as briskly as his spacesuit allowed, kicking stones out of his way until he reached the path the robot had cleared on his first visit to the ship. He suddenly felt very alone under the black canopy of distant stars overhead.

Arriving at the central cylindrical support, Dmitri commenced his brilliant strategy for boarding the vessel. He began pounding the sky blue outer surface of the cylinder. To his dismay, no hatchway appeared in the smooth surface. Even more alarming: his furious pounding produced no discernable sounds. He heard himself scream into the empty solitude of his spacesuit. Had he risked everything to be left outside the ship in the freezing Martian atmosphere? Would he be carted back to base by one of Kaminsky's lackeys to face charges of endangering corporate property and insubordination?

The pursuing rover wheeled into view from around the curve in the crater wall. Dmitri waved at it. He wondered who Kaminsky had sent after him. The rover kept approaching.

"Can we talk about this?" Dmitri called out over his intercom.

The rover kept rolling towards him.

"Who's in there? C'mon. Let's talk."

When no response came, prickly fingers of fear gripped him in the gut. *Damn you, Kaminsky. You won't even let me plead my case.*

"Hey, stop." *One more appeal to reason.*

No luck. The rover wheeled inexorably towards him.

*What the fuck. I guess we all abandoned reason when we signed up for this.*

Dmitri backed up against the outer wall of the cylinder. *I should run. Why am I not jumping in the rover and booking? Because I can't live in the damn thing indefinitely. Sooner or later, the Martian atmosphere or one of my esteemed co-workers will catch up with me.*

The rover bore down on him—only a few meters away now. *This is it. I'll be squashed like a bug.*

And then he fell backward.

Bright colored light blinded him. *I'm inside the cylinder.* Something broke his fall. He felt the disc and its familiar energy field supporting him—moving him up inside the cylinder. Light—every color in the spectrum—danced around him.

"Oh shit. No brakes. It's pulling me in."

The voice coming through his comm link sounded familiar. Dmitri looked down. He had company—the pursuing rover. *Now what?*

He lost consciousness.

* * *

He awoke staring up at the giant caretaker robot looming over him. It had removed his spacesuit. He moved his hands over the surface around him. It felt like warm glass. No white table supported him this time.

A row of contoured structures towered above him along what he considered to be the main deck where the robot had apparently deposited him. He estimated the ceiling height at somewhere between twenty and thirty meters—a big ship. How many passengers did it carry? Then, he remembered what the robot had told him on his first visit. Most of the living quarters had been removed. The ship only carried a crew of eight, plus the caretaker robot.

The structures behind the robot fascinated him. They looked like storage bins that measured two-meters high by a meter wide and rose from the deck like mini-skyscrapers of four units each. Their color pulsed from purple to grayish blue, as if they were breathing, like the walls of the ship. With no ladders in sight, he wondered how the crew reached the higher units. *Can they telekinetically open the units and remove what they want?*

He gazed briefly at the circle of sleep pods some twenty meters away near the interior curved wall of the ship. The robot offered him a hand. He grasped it and stood. He turned to examine his surroundings. No darkness obscured his view—no secrets, this time. He noticed oval openings in a few of the storage bins. Oddly shaped silver tools, multicolored vials, and rolls of gray mesh material littered the deck around the openings. Signs of work in progress, Dmitri figured.

"Are those storage bins?" Dmitri asked, pointing to the nearest row.

"*Yes.*"

"It looks like the rows go on forever."

"*The storage units occupy most of the main deck. They hold supplies for the crew, replacement parts for the ship, and parts to be reassembled into big terraforming machines. Over half the bins are empty because we are not carrying our full complement of passengers. As I told you on your first visit, the open space above the bins all the way to the ceiling is large enough to accommodate living quarters and stasis pods for twenty-four hundred citizens.*"

The robot led him to the nest of sleep pods. He noticed that it had shed the tread carriage it used for traction. It probably used the treads and power-arms for strenuous work outside and about the ship. He admired the unit's adaptability.

The circle of eight pods greeted him in the same condition that he had left them on his first visit.

An oval console rose from the center of the circle. The circle opened towards Dmitri. With an open palm swept towards the opening, the robot invited Dmitri into the circle.

"Is the ship alive? Does it have a consciousness like me?"

The robot entered the circle. "*I have learned your language sufficiently. In a moment, I will speak to you aloud.*"

And then the robot spoke to him. *Remarkable*, Dmitri thought. *It sounds almost human. It picked up every subtlety in my voice.*

"Every fiber of the ship is imbued with an artificial intelligence far beyond your own. You might say it is an artificial living being. That is the best description I can give you."

"If the ship is so smart, why hasn't it fixed the problem with the sleep pods?"

"Because I have not allowed the ship to access the control panel."

"What?"

"The ship is a danger to the passengers. It is my responsibility to protect them."

"Why is the ship a danger to the crew?"

"The ship is malfunctioning. It may kill the crew if I let it awaken them."

"Why haven't you awakened them?"

"The system is defective. Both of the backup systems are also defective. The ship won't allow me to access the control panel and I have blocked the ship's access. We are at an impasse. Please help me to awaken the crew."

"How can you expect *me* to awaken the passengers?"

"My sub-routines tell me you can if you follow directions"

The robot turned. Dmitri watched it march towards one of the contoured bins. It placed a finger on the front surface. An oval opening appeared. It extracted equipment from the cabinet and dropped each item methodically onto the deck of the ship. The silver tools clattered and clanked, bouncing once or twice before coming to rest haphazardly.

*This robot is either a klutz or it's gone mad,* he thought.

*"Follow my instructions. I will show you what to do."*

Dmitri thought the robot was talking to him telepathically again. Then he remembered it had begun speaking to him out loud in a voice that sounded like his. Was the subconscious mind of one of the crew members speaking to him from the sleep pods? The voice sounded strong, self-confident, and warm, despite its formal tone. It reminded him of his father's voice speaking to him as a young boy when they took long walks in the hills overlooking the Dnieper River near their home in Smolensk.

*"I am the ship. The robot is disturbed, as you can see. I used it to bring you here. I used subtle commands to make the robot think it was responding to its own programming. Please don't speak aloud again. The robot is unstable and unreliable. We must be careful. Please move slowly and follow my instructions.*

*"Can't you shut the robot down?"*

*"No. It has activated its autonomous behavioral programming. These programs are only supposed to be used if I am disabled. The robot thinks I am malfunctioning, and therefore it ignores my commands. I can only affect it with subtle, disguised suggestions."*

*"Did you hypnotize or program me when I came aboard the first time?"*

*"I spoke to your subconscious mind to appeal to your better instincts. I made no attempts to control your behavior. You are acting under your own free will."*

He had to choose whether to believe the robot or the ship. Watching the robot sloppily spill the contents of a storage cabinet onto the deck did not do much to inspire his confidence. Instinct told him to go with the ship, although he knew full well that both the robot and the ship might be off their rockers. He knew something else: unless someone intervened soon, the crew members were goners.

The ship instructed him to leave the pod circle and venture off to a cluster of supply bins several rows behind the robot's location. Dmitri succeeded in doing so without arousing the robot's attention. He collected several items from one of the bins: a large vial of pale pink liquid, a foot-long syringe, scissors, and a bulky roll of cloth mesh. He felt like a child in a giant's castle.

The ship directed him to another location away from the sleep pods.

*"I can't carry any more,"* Dmitri complained.

*"I am not asking you to get more supplies. I am directing you to your co-worker. The supplies are for him, not the passengers."*

Dmitri had forgotten about his pursuer. *"My co-worker tried to kill me. I'd much rather help the crew first."*

*"Your co-worker requires immediate attention. Please follow my instructions."*

*Your artificial heart is bigger than mine,* Dmitri thought. He had to follow the ship's instructions, even if he didn't agree with them. If he wasted time arguing, the crew might die.

Dmitri journeyed beyond the rows of contoured bins containing supplies and hardware systems beyond anything his tiny mind could imagine. He passed banks of clear tubing intertwined like giant ropes feeding into an oblong dome rising out of the center of the deck.

The dome looked to be about fifty meters long. He guessed that the ship's engine compartment rested underneath the golden dome. The golden color pulsed like the bin colors, alternatively growing pale and rich in luster. The sight of the glowing dome registered as nothing short of majestic. Maybe the builders of this ship embodied the same majesty. Or maybe they were cold-blooded killers like the person who tried to squish him outside the cylinder. Maybe the aliens needed a soft-hearted patsy like him to further their evil purposes.

*I should go. Right now.* Then he thought: *What makes you think the ship will let you leave?*

He found the rover turned on its side behind the far side of the golden dome. Jon Henderson lay sprawled up against it, unconscious, with a ragged gash in his space helmet. His old friend Hollywood Henderson had come to kill him. He wanted badly to let Henderson die.

*"What happened here?"* Dmitri asked the ship.

*"The caretaker unit attacked your co-worker when it learned this person meant to harm you. The robot interpreted any threat to you as a threat to the crew."*

*"Because I am their only hope?"*

*"Yes. Shall we get to work?"*

*"Why am I helping someone who came here to kill me?"*

*"Because it is wrong to let him die, and we may need him."*

*"You don't know this guy as well as I do, but I'm not going to waste time arguing."*

Dmitri's skills as a healer left much to be desired. Fortunately, the ship told him what to do. He removed Henderson's suit, injected him with a dose of the pink liquid, and then cleaned, shaved, sutured, and dressed the head wound. The ship calculated the right dosage of medicine for Henderson's body. The heavy gauge of the syringe's needle made administering the injection a challenge, but Dmitri managed to pull it off with the ship talking him through the procedure.

He left Henderson still unconscious and resting on the deck of the ship, out of harm's way. Henderson had a lot of explaining to do when they got off the ship—assuming they got off it.

# Chapter 17

# MARS—ALIEN SHIP

DMITRI APPROACHED THE circle of sleep pods. The caretaker robot waited for him in the opening leading to the oval control panel in the center of the circle. For all he knew, the alien crew might already be dead. The pitch-black color of each massive pod yielded no clues as to the condition of its occupants. The ship or the robot had allowed him a glimpse of the female crew member in stasis. That glimpse had brought him back to the ship against his better judgment.

Maybe the ship had brainwashed him into coming back. It had said otherwise, but the idea struck him as a distinct possibility. He had to be out of his mind to think he could outwit and outmaneuver the immensely powerful and super intelligent caretaker robot.

He waited for the robot to move out of the way. It stood its ground. Two small ovals opened in its head—eyes as black and bottomless as the sleep pods. If he saw any light in those eyes, it might be the last light he ever saw.

"I have detected that the ship has been speaking to you. You must not listen to anything the ship tells you. The ship is a danger to the crew."

"Why would the ship want to harm the crew?"

"I have detected a malfunction in the ship's computers."

"Isn't it possible that you are both impaired?"

"I have run diagnostics on my systems. I am not malfunctioning."

"Okay. Let's get started."

"You may enter. If the ship speaks to you, do not listen."

Fortunately, the ship had already provided him with all the information he needed to address the breakdown in the reanimation system and its two backup systems. Essentially, he was going to create a third backup system. But what if he got stuck?

"I'll need some tools to do this," he told the robot. "Please bring me the ones on the deck over there."

He pointed to the tools the robot had spilled out of the supply bins about fifty meters across from their location. He didn't need them, but Dmitri thought that if the ship spoke to him, then maybe the robot would be too far away to pick up the conversation.

A faint light glimmered in the robot's dread eyes.

*Shit. It thinks I'm a threat.*

The light began to swirl in a lazy circle inside those eyes. Dmitri had seen enough. He bolted towards the rows of storage bins that lined the main deck like a field of corn.

The ship directed him to a row of bins near the wall of the fuselage opposite the sleep pods. One of the bins opened, revealing a rack of shiny objects. One end of the long-barreled objects tapered into a handle. They stood at a forty-five-degree angle in the rack. The latches securing them snapped open. Dmitri grabbed one. He tilted the barrel towards him. Two round holes peered at him from the other end. It was clearly a weapon—one made for larger hands than his—but lightweight.

"*Point the barrel of the weapon at your target,*" the ship told him. "*Push the button on the right side of the handle. Paint your target with the laser and push the left-hand button to fire.*"

He liked these aliens. They made easy-to-use technology. The procedure to repair the stasis system and revive the crew didn't seem too hard, and the ship would be there to help him, if necessary. The only thing standing in his way was a gigantic homicidal robot.

He heard the heavy *squish* of robotic boots behind a nearby row of bins. *The caretaker robot—ha. It sure as hell wants to take care of me.*

Dmitri readied his weapon.

A cluster of bins exploded to Dmitri's right. The robot crunched through the debris. Slowly, it turned towards him.

He pushed the right-hand button.

The pale blue light in the robot's eyes darkened into purple and then indigo. Any second now, it would fire an unearthly, deadly blast at him.

Dmitri pushed the left-hand button. The weapon vibrated. A blue beam shot out of the other end. He felt the recoil. It almost knocked him backward.

A blinding flash of blue light issued from the robot's eyes. Simultaneously, its body rocked sideways while its right arm exploded into splinters.

The energy blast intended to pulverize Dmitri disintegrated half the row of bins to his left, instead. Something inside one of the bins exploded.

While the robot recovered from the shock of losing an arm, Dmitri ran wildly; as fast and as far as his legs would carry him. When the adrenaline rush subsided, he found himself back at the upturned rover. He expected to find his former friend lying where he had left him, in a foul mood. Instead, there was no trace of Hollywood Henderson.

He heard the robot's boots against the deck again, and then a series of explosions. He prayed the robot had not decided to blow up the ship. He saw plumes of smoke and parts of storage bins raining down from the empty space below the high ceiling. *The damn thing is on a rampage.*

The mad robot appeared suddenly, trapping him in a narrow alleyway between the long golden dome and the hull of the ship.

"*Don't use your weapon. The caretaker unit is too close to the propulsion system.*"

He had figured the golden dome topped off the ship's engine compartment. *Brilliant deduction. Too bad it won't save my ass.*

*"Any suggestions?"* Dmitri asked the ship.

As if to answer, the golden dome glowed a bright orange. The rogue robot jolted to a halt in mid-step.

*"The energy surge from the engines has temporarily disabled the robot. You can approach the unit now. I will tell you how to permanently shut it down."*

*"I'm on it."* Dmitri felt every muscle in his body relax.

*"First, you'll need some tools."*

*"More tools?"*

*"Yes. Please hurry."*

Heeding the ship's voice inside his head, Dmitri collected two multi-purpose tools. He had to walk all the way back to the first row of bins near the sleep pods to pick up the instruments. He passed bin clusters that had been reduced to glistening shards, reminding him of confetti embers. He guessed the robot had blown up the bins in a demented rage after losing its arm. He wondered what had thrown its programming so far off track.

The size of the tools and his weapon made them difficult to carry despite their lightweight construction. As he passed the last row of contoured bins, Jon Henderson stepped out from behind the nearest cluster. Henderson held a weapon like the one he held in his left hand. He dropped the tools. Henderson pointed the business end of the weapon at him before Dmitri had a chance to scoot his weapon over into his right hand.

"I'm really pissed at Kaminsky for sending me on this fool's errand. I have a bad headache, too."

"I don't feel sorry for you, Jon."

"Kaminsky knows you're here. I told him before the robot knocked my lights out. Drop your weapon."

"No. I'm taking you back to base."

"It's not happening, bozo. If I drop my weapon, you'll shoot me. You think I forgot that you tried to kill me outside of the ship?"

Dmitri switched the weapon into his right hand and leveled it at Henderson.

"I know how to use this thing," Henderson warned.

"Did you blow up any storage bins learning?"

"A few. It was kind of a trial and error thing. The robot did most of the damage."

"You idiot. What if you blew up something vital to the crew's survival?"

"All you care about is the damn alien crew. You just haul off and leave *your* crew out to dry."

"So now we blow each other to bits?"

Henderson extended his arm and the weapon.

The big holes pointed straight at Dmitri's head. He hit the deck and rolled, aiming his weapon at Henderson's chest.

"Aw, fuck this." Henderson lowered his weapon. "I never wanted to kill you."

"That's big of you."

Henderson hung his head and stared at the deck. "The hell with Kaminsky and that asshole Caliphas."

Dmitri rose slowly from the deck with his gun trained on Henderson.

"Give me your weapon."

Henderson handed it over.

Grabbing Henderson by his shoulder lapel, Dmitri said, "C'mon, knucklehead. Let's take a walk and put the big bad robot out of its misery."

With his eyes still glued on the deck, Henderson said nothing.

Together, they trudged away.

## Chapter 18

# MARS—ALIEN SHIP

IF ONLY THEY could have simply switched the damn robot off. No, that would have been too easy. Once its systems recovered from the energy surge of the engines, the ship told them, the robot had the capability of switching itself back on. As it turned out, the ship had worse news to deliver: they had a measly ten minutes to complete the intricate shutdown procedure.

With access to the governing CPU in the robot's head, the procedure would have been faster and easier. Unfortunately, the top down option wasn't available, thanks to their puny stature and the lack of a suitable ladder. Dmitri and Henderson had to perform the shutdown from the ball in the middle of the unit's torso. Despite guidance and encouragement from the ship, both men found it difficult to operate in the cramped cavity beneath the unit's protective exoskeleton.

"This tool is hard to work with," Henderson complained. "My arms and hands hurt."

"The tools are made for bigger hands and stronger bodies. We can only work with the hands we were dealt."

"I'm starting to regret my decision to let you live."

Dmitri ignored Henderson and his own aching, exhausted body.

Besides a raw desire to save his own skin, his concern for the passengers propelled him to complete the difficult shutdown process. Every minute that passed put the lives of the crew in deeper peril. Maybe the ship had foreseen he would need Henderson's help to deactivate the robot. It had told him to pick up *two* tools. Dmitri had thought they were for different purposes. Now he noticed that they looked exactly alike. The ship had calculated the low probability of Dmitri and Henderson bumping each other off, probably based on their friendship—the one that, by the way, no longer existed. Evidently, it had access to the contents of his mind. He marveled at the ship's artificial intelligence. It had a depth, breadth, and subtlety that humans could only dream of.

Following the ship's instructions, they worked on the robot from opposite sides. Dmitri cut through a tissue deep inside the ball. A second later, the pale light inside the ball turned blood red in color. He instinctively pulled his hands out of the open cavity.

"It's going to self-destruct. Open the hatch. Let us out of here," Henderson shouted at the ship.

"There is no danger," the ship told them. It had been communicating with them telepathically. Now it spoke vocally, apparently to calm Henderson down.

"The red light is a warning that the robot's systems are close to critical impairment. The red light is good news."

"You coulda fooled me," Henderson found it necessary to say.

They resumed probing deeply inside the robot's body.

Without warning, the red light inside the torso began to pulsate.

"I will self-destruct in three minutes." the robot said. "Please clear the area."

"Steady now," the ship assured them in a confident tone. "We're almost there. We've cleared the way to the manual deactivation terminal. Dmitri, you need to press each corner of the blue plastic square in front of you to open the terminal."

"You didn't say anything about a self-destruct mechanism," Dmitri said.

"I didn't want to make you nervous. You can walk away to a safe distance and hear the robot blow up. The explosion will wreck my engine compartment beyond repair. If any of the crew members survive, they'll never be able to go home again."

"I'm outta here."

"Go back to the main deck area, Jon Henderson. You will be safe there."

"We're wasting time," Dmitri said to the ship. "I have the terminal open. I see a keyboard with characters in your language."

"Press the third key from the right in the top row."

Humming the Star-Spangled Banner, Dmitri pressed the key.

The ship gave him instructions to press five more keys.

"One minute to self-destruct," the robot announced. Dmitri doubted he had enough time to make it to safety if he bolted.

"One more key, Dmitri. Press the fourth key from the left on the bottom row."

*Don't screw this up.* He pressed the last key.

The pulsing of the red light accelerated until it became a blur.

*Oh shit.*

Dmitri stuck his fingers in his ears. A reflex—a lot of good it would do.

The blue plastic faceplate of the terminal slid shut. Dmitri waited to be blown to kingdom come.

"Self-destruct sequence aborted," the robot said.

Silence. The red light stopped flashing. The torso cavity darkened.

"Congratulations, Dmitri. You deactivated the robot."

"Don't ask me to do anything like that again."

"I will try not to."

"What do we do now?"

"Decide what to do with Jon Henderson. It's your call."

Dmitri walked the distance back to the main deck, debating Jon Henderson's fate. *Should I kill him? I want to kill him. Fuck. How can I kill him, even if he deserves it?*

He made his way through the rows of shattered and intact bins to the main deck area. There he found Jon Henderson sprawled on the floor, staring at the distant ceiling.

He walked up to Henderson and kicked him in the side. Groaning, Henderson sat up.

"You piece of shit. I should kill you. You deserve to die for being a coward and a low-life and a scumbag."

"I love you too, Semerov. What the fuck was I supposed to do? If I don't do what Kaminsky says, it's my ass. I'm sorry. When push comes to shove, I'm always going to save my own ass over someone else's."

"You're pathetic, but you can be useful. Do you want to be useful?"

"What's my other choice?"

"I break your skull and put you in a sleep pod for the rest of eternity after I wake up the passengers."

"You wouldn't do that."

"Try me. The ship will back me up on anything I decide to do with you."

"Okay. Okay. What do I have to do?"

"You grab a few hours of sleep and then take the rover back to the base."

"Yeah, sure, and get myself impaled for not killing you. No thanks."

"Let me finish. You'll tell them I'm dead. We had a fight. You killed me. I bashed you in the head and the robot fixed you up."

"What will you do here?"

"I'll figure it out."

"Why can't I stay here with you? This whole gig is way out of control. I didn't sign up to become a cold-blooded killer."

"I'm touched, Hollywood, but Kaminsky will send more people if you don't go back."

"Maybe we can fight them with the help of the alien crew. I'll bet our guys are no match for these fuckers if they're anything like this ship they built."

"We have no idea what the crew will do once we awaken them."

"Then what the fuck are you doing waking them up?"

"Something tells me it's the right thing to do."

"They might be bad asses."

"Get some rest, Hollywood. You look like hell."

"You don't look so hot yourself." Henderson pulled himself up from the floor to face Dmitri. "I can't go back to base."

"Just keep your head down. Pretend you're still one of them. We'll get through this standing up. I promise."

"You better know what you're doing."

Dmitri wished he did.

"I'll show you to the sleeping quarters," the ship said to Henderson.

A disc appeared underneath Henderson's feet. An energy field that looked like crystal glass surrounded him.

"Stand still and don't look down," the ship said.

"The ship thinks of everything, Hollywood. You're in good hands."

Despite the encouragement, Henderson did not look happy.

*Always the reluctant hero,* Dmitri thought, while the strange elevator carried Henderson high above his head. When it neared what he thought of as the second floor, an opening appeared and the disc disappeared into it.

Finally, it was time to awaken the crew. He felt drained and at the same time excited. He wanted to meet these aliens. As a boy, he had always dreamed of encountering alien races. Now his dreams had materialized. Maybe.

As he walked back to the sleeping pods, the ship spoke to him.

"I know it has been a long day for you."

Dmitri burst out laughing. "That's a major understatement...uh, do you have a name?"

"Call me Arcon. My real name is a symbol that only the crew can understand. Speaking for myself and the crew; thank you for the sacrifices you have made to help us. Are you ready to awaken the crew?"

He wanted badly to meet the crew members. At the same time, he felt a nagging concern for his well-being, and the well-being of every living thing back on Earth. What if these aliens turned out to be a bunch of storm troopers? What he did next would affect the course of human history, for better or worse. *I'm gonna be a hero or the biggest jackass the world has ever known.*

"Let's do it," he said.

He entered the circle of sleep pods. It felt surreal to finally be doing this, but he also felt bone tired. Like the ship said: it had been a very long day. *Maybe I should get some rest. I'm in no shape to meet a bunch of intergalactic space travelers.* Then he thought: *Maybe there isn't time to rest.*

The ship interrupted his thoughts. "I can do most of the work to restore the stasis systems. You only need to execute a simple routine to allow me access to the control panel. Then you can join your co-worker for some rest upstairs."

"He's not my co-worker."

"As you wish. Shall we proceed?"

Arcon told him how to unlock the control panel and enter a sequence of commands to restore its access to the stasis system.

"I'll take it from here. Please step outside of the circle. Your presence might startle the awakeners."

Dmitri left the circle. Arcon directed him to a work station ten meters outside of it. Happy to be off his feet, he sat in an oversized chair with comfortable padding and an unobstructed view of the stasis pods.

Light appeared at the bottom of each pod. At first, the pods looked to Dmitri like large soup tureens cooking on a giant electric oven. Then the light crept up the sides of each pod until the passengers inside became visible amid the gaseous atmosphere.

He watched in fascination as a halo of golden light surrounded each pod.

Dmitri assumed the light was an energetic catalyst in the awakening process. Soon the pods would open and he'd watch the crew members emerge.

"I'm scanning the health condition of each crew member."

Scolding himself for assuming anything, especially something related to advanced alien technology, Dmitri waited for Arcon to complete its examination.

"I'm sorry to say that we've lost five passengers."

"They're dead?"

"Yes. We split the system into two sets of four units each to reduce the chances of losing the entire crew in case of a malfunction. One of the sets failed completely. Three of the four passengers survived in the other set."

"Only three out of eight survived?"

"I'm afraid so."

The news of the five deaths hit him like a shockwave. And then Dmitri watched the pods open.

# Chapter 19

# MARS—MINING BASE

"I'LL WALK YOU back to your quarters," Logan offered. There was something he wanted to air out with Kate after their latest meeting with Rashawn and Kaneko. It had mostly to do with her attitude. And there was something else—something big.

They strolled past the medical bays lining the hallway leading away from Kaneko's office. Moving confidently with her head held high, Kate kept her eyes looking straight ahead, as if no one accompanied her.

"Are you angry with me for keeping you confined to the base?"

"I resent your motherly concern about my health."

"I take exception to the 'motherly' reference. Kaneko gave you medical orders, not recommendations. I'm not a doctor. I'm not going to go against the judgment of the best physician this side of the moon and one of the best astronaut specialists in the world."

"I'm not questioning Kaneko's judgment. It's your responsibility to see the big picture and let me do my job."

They passed the recreation room where two of Kaminsky's software engineers played a spirited game of ping pong. Logan said nothing until they entered the hallway leading to Kate's quarters.

"Don't tell me how to do *my* job, Kate. Your life is more important to me than our mission here."

"If I want to risk my life, then I should be able to risk it."

"I'm going to slap you upside the head and put you back in the medical bay if you keep up this stubborn attitude. You really are pissing me off."

They reached the door to Kate's quarters.

"I suggest you spend more time thinking about what you *can do* rather than complaining about your doctor's orders."

"We're not done with this conversation. Come inside."

"I have things to do and nothing more to say."

"Come inside."

Reluctantly, Logan followed Kate into her quarters. Photos of Kate as an undergraduate student posing with friends and satellite photos of Mars at various altitudes plastered the walls of the cramped quarters. A small work table, clothes closet, and narrow bunk bed comprised the Spartan elements of the room. As Commander, Logan enjoyed a few more feet of living space in his quarters. Notwithstanding the extra space, a room at a budget motel was a five-star hotel suite in comparison.

Standing alone with Kate in the cramped surroundings gave him goose bumps. He didn't have time to feel uncomfortable because she took one step forward and kissed him passionately.

He broke away from her. "Are you trying to seduce me so I'll let you leave the base?"

She slapped him hard across the face.

"I guess not. What are you doing?"

"I'm tired of the sexual tension between us. I know you feel it."

Yes, he had felt it, but he had kept it at arms-length. Now it grabbed him with the arms of a vampire lover in the dead of night. The black tar rose from the pit to pull him down; deeper down.

He took her in his arms and kissed her. As they embraced, he felt her pulling him toward the bunk bed.

"We can't do this."

"I know," she said.

He unzipped her jumpsuit and she unzipped his. Awkwardly, amid kissing and the frenzied caressing of exposed flesh, they managed to wriggle out of their outer garments. In their underwear, they wrestled for a comfortable position on the bunk.

"My bed's not big enough," she whispered into his ear.

Slipping off the bunk, he pulled her upright. They stood toe to toe and nose to nose.

Pain and desire roiled his insides. The darkness in the pit of his soul beckoned.

"We could lose our commissions," he said, and then began removing her sports bra.

"Nobody's watching," she said, and practically ripped off his undershirt.

The black void closed around him. There was no up—no down.

He kissed her deeply and removed her panties while she removed his briefs. Leaping into his arms, her legs encircled his waist. He entered her. They pushed against each other, trying to make their love last. As his ardor rose, she moaned in ecstatic pleasure.

"Oh my God," she whispered into his ear. "Don't stop."

Logan slowed his thrusting movements until he thought he would lose his mind. When he couldn't hold himself any longer, he exploded inside of her. He felt Kate climax as her legs gripped him tighter. With one final kiss, their joy abated. The fire of their love turned to embers, and then to ashes. Their sudden passion left no room for an afterglow.

She slipped off him and began to gather her clothing, as if the act might undo what they had just done. Following her lead, he gathered his randomly discarded clothing, dressing quickly to cover the shame of his nakedness and the horrible emptiness inside.

He watched Kate finish dressing. Zipping up her jumpsuit, she turned to him.

"Are you okay?"

"Yes and no."

I know what you mean."

*No, you don't.*

Her expression changed.

"Is something wrong?"

"I keep having dreams that I'm being watched," she said. "There are times I get the creepy feeling I'm not alone in the privacy of my own room."

"Kaminsky and his people are keeping close tabs on everything we do. Try not to let it get too far under your skin."

"I let you get too far under my skin."

Taking refuge in his Strong Commander role, he laughed and placed his hands on her shoulders. "I think this needed to happen. I felt the tension between us the moment we met. Something tells me we're going to have to depend on each other to survive here. I'm glad we cleared the space between us. I think we're going to have to trust each other deeply and instinctually."

She pushed him away. "So, having sex with me was purely a utilitarian exercise?"

"No. I didn't mean it that way. I suppose I'm out of practice with intimacy. I've had only one deep relationship with a woman and that goes back to my college days. I really haven't made room for anyone since then." *And while we're on the subject, I'm afraid of the dark.*

"I haven't fully trusted a boyfriend since I was fourteen years old. His parents tore us apart when they found out we had become intimate. We stayed in touch secretly because we had so much in common, and then his parents became missionaries and moved to China."

She came closer and allowed him to hold her. "Not that I consider you a boyfriend, but it seems like we have things in common. Maybe a lot of things."

"Yeah. We had to come to Mars and fall apart under all this stress to find out."

"I just thought of something," she said. "I can show you how to take the readings at the mine and do the other tests. We can use a live video feed to make sure you do everything right. It's so obvious. Why didn't we think of it before?"

"I thought of it, but I was pretty sure you'd say no."

"I think you're right. My professional pride would have been in the way."

"I intended to mention it to you before you invited me in and my mind went missing in action."

"I'll take that as a compliment."

"There's something else I want to tell you. Keep it between us."

"You love me to pieces."

"Stop it. Kaneko carbon dated those cell samples she showed us. She's repeating the tests because the results make no sense. If she gets the same results, it looks like the cells aren't millions of years old. They're only a few decades old."

"What?"

"I know. It points to three possibilities: first, intelligent life existed here up until very recently."

"Or life still exists here somewhere underground."

"Right. Or the third possibility: aliens visited Mars not too long ago, and something bad happened to them."

"This is mind-blowing. I can see why Kaneko is double-checking her results."

They went on talking about Kaneko's discovery and its world-shaking implications, unaware that a miniature camera was recording every word and image from inside an air-conditioning duct above the photos on Kate's wall.

# Chapter 20

# MARS—ALIEN SHIP

TWO WOMEN AND a man emerged from the pods. The first thing that struck him was their height. All three of them stood preternaturally tall. The woman closest to Dmitri had long, russet-colored hair that had grown down to her thighs. She was the statuesque beauty he had glimpsed the first time he had boarded the ship at the robot's invitation. She glared at him with dark green eyes, unashamed of her nakedness and apparently unafraid of his presence. She had a muscular body that nonetheless maintained an alluring, feminine presence. Dmitri wondered how she had kept her muscle tone in stasis. Somehow, the deep-sleep system kept the crew exercised, but it didn't cut hair. *Maybe it's another malfunction, or maybe just an oversight. At least we know these aliens aren't perfect.*

The second woman appeared more classically feminine, with red hair and brown eyes. Like the first woman, she stared at him with unblinking eyes and an open expression. He wondered if they were reading his mind. Both of them looked human in every detail, except for their height and the six digits on their hands and feet.

"Hello," he said. "May I get you some clothes, or maybe a pair of scissors?"

The women made no reply, continuing instead to stare at him; evaluating him, he felt certain.

"I came here to help awaken you," Dmitri offered with the friendliest smile he could muster in the unsettling presence of two butt-naked, gorgeous Amazons somewhere between seven and eight feet tall.

The first women opened her mouth and coughed up a greenish yellow liquid. She proceeded to expel more liquid in long, wracking coughs, accompanied by the second woman and the male crew member. The man had curly blue hair that was not overgrown, and pale blue eyes with a black dot in the middle. His slender, muscular body heaved with the effort to dispel the stasis fluids and mucous in his lungs and windpipe. Dmitri found the male's coloring and lack of hair growth perplexing. His height and unrelenting glare made him the scariest of the trio.

After a few minutes, the three crew members regained their composure and stood on their pods, looking at him. He wished like hell they would say something.

The muscular woman jumped to the floor and the other two followed her lead. She moved off towards the supply bins, followed by the other woman. The male stayed behind, trying his best, it seemed, to look threatening. Like the women, he appeared human, except for the hair and eyes. And then Dmitri noticed that he had a mound where his genitals belonged. *He isn't a he,* Dmitri thought. *He's an it, and it looks like it wants to kick my ass.*

"Why am I standing here with this unfriendly guy staring at me?"

"*Be patient,*" the ship said, reverting back to telepathic communication. "*The women are going off to make themselves presentable. They left this fellow behind to keep an eye on you. His name is Galatar.*"

"*Is he artificial?*" Dmitri asked, choosing to speak telepathically so as not to piss Galatar off.

"*Our deep space travelers have the option of choosing to extend their lives and careers in old age with a substitute bionic body, but the consciousness remains intact. Galatar has chosen this option. He functions as an engineer, systems analyst, and practically anything else we ask him to do. His coloring is different to distinguish him from the general population aboard colony ships and on our home world."*

*"He looks mean"*

*"He's not mean. Galatar has a strong desire to protect his crew mates. He'll start warming up to you when Silenna returns. She's the pilot, second engineer, strategist, and team leader. As we speak, I'm updating Silenna and Elora on everything that's happened since the ship landed. Elora is an Astrobiologist and a Geologist. She can also fly the ship and is responsible for looking after me."*

*"You have a talented crew. Tell me about the ones who perished."*

*"We lost three soldiers and two habitat and agricultural specialists. Half the crew had military training, including Silenna, in case we learned our ships were destroyed by hostile forces here. I've learned from you that our ships crash-landed for no apparent reason. I've informed the others of this."*

While they waited for Elora and Silenna to return, Galatar kept up his unfriendly routine with the piercing stare and expressionless face. He wondered if the freak was reading his mind.

*"Don't worry. The crew members can't read your mind. Only I can."*

*"That's a relief,"* he said with a trace of sarcasm. *"How will I speak with them?"*

*"The conversation will go through me. I'll translate for both sides. It will seem as though you are talking directly to one another."*

As Dmitri reflected in disbelief on each step that had brought him to this precarious moment, the women returned. Elora and Silenna appeared in black sequined, body-hugging jump suits and medium heeled boots covered in a padded orange material. Silenna had trimmed her unkempt hair and drawn it back in a ponytail reaching halfway down her long, arching back. Elora wore her hair loosely in curls down to her shoulders. Both women had applied light-blue facial makeup and had accented their eyes with liberal dabs of purple eye shadow. The women had pruned their fingernails to male lengths; presumably to accommodate whatever work projects lay ahead. They looked light years beyond presentable. The effect on him was utterly heart stopping.

Silenna approached him. Dmitri noticed she walked a bit woodenly.

*"I'm recovering from the effects of prolonged deep sleep,"* she said telepathically, courtesy of Arcon's intermediary translation.

*"No need for you to feel self-conscious,"* Dmitri managed to reply while he struggled to adjust to the intimidating presence of a woman fully two feet taller than himself and so powerfully and alluringly built. From behind, Elora and Galatar walked off together. Arcon informed Dmitri that Elora and Galatar had work to do.

The gargantuan Silenna teetered on her feet as she drew closer. He offered a hand to steady her, but she made no attempt to accept it. Regaining her balance, she glared at him, as before.

*I'm breakfast food,* he thought.

*"What are you called?"*

*"Dmitri...Semerov."*

*"I am Silenna."*

He extended his hand to shake hers, and then withdrew it when she looked at it, as if thinking: *why is he poking his hand in mid-air at me?*

She took a step backwards and continued to study him without showing a hint emotion.

*"Sorry. We have a custom of shaking hands when we meet new people. It was purely a reflex."*

To his profound relief, her features softened and she broke into a faint smile. *"Elora, Galatar and I are deeply grateful for your efforts to revive us. Although we are saddened by the loss of our crew members, we thank you for saving the three of us and our mission."*

*"I felt compelled to help you. Unfortunately, I did so against the wishes of my co-workers. I'm afraid you can't trust the team of mining colonists here and the people they answer to back on Earth."*

*"If that is so, it will complicate our mission. We came here to locate and study the remains of our ships...and terraform the planet."*

*"Terraforming the planet will affect our colonies."*

"*Of course. We did not expect to find two colonies of your people here. I offer you my assurances that we intend to cooperate fully with the colonists and assist them in reaching their goals while we reach ours.*"

"*I'm sure the colony we call Mars One will welcome your presence. The mining colonists view your presence here as a problem. They think you are asleep. They have no intentions of cooperating with you. My co-worker came here to kill me. He has changed his mind, obviously. I think it would be best to send him back to the colony to report me dead and to confirm that the ship's crew remains asleep. Whatever you decide to do, it's best to keep the element of surprise on your side.*"

"*Why are the mining colonists hostile?*"

"*They don't want media coverage. If your presence here is revealed, it will generate an explosion of coverage and raise questions.*"

Her expression turned contemplative. "*Thank you. I'll have to talk to Arcon and my crew before deciding what to do.*"

The walls of the ship came alive with light. A series of thin rectangular shapes, rounded at the edges, slid into the room from the walls. The shapes measured about six feet long by four feet high and a foot wide. Multicolored blocks of text and graphs populated the screens inside the rectangles.

The sudden changes unnerved Dmitri. Silenna responded to his agitation.

"*The ship has a backup intelligence system. Elora has deployed it to replace the primary AI while we check for malfunctions.*"

"*It saved all of us. I'd say it's working.*"

Silenna made no reply.

"*May I ask you a few questions?*"

Silenna nodded.

"*What's the name of your home world?*"

"*We call it Aneleya in your language. It means 'giver of everything to everyone.' It was once a paradise before the age of our dying twin suns.*"

"*Will you be able to repair your ship?*"

"*I don't know. Please excuse me. Arcon says I am needed to help Elora and Galatar assess the damage. You look like you need rest. Would you like to go upstairs to the crew quarters?*"

"*Yes. Thank you. I'm exhausted.*"

Silenna smiled at him. "*I'll show you to the lift, Dmitri Semerov.*"

# Chapter 21

# MARS—NORTH FACE MINE

FROM THE MOUTH of the north face mine, Logan watched the brute machine tear chunks out of the wall of the crater and gobble the hard rocks down like swathes of flesh from the flank of an animal.

"It's show time," Logan said.

Rashawn touched the holster of the energy weapon tethered to his right hip. "I'm ready to dance," he said.

The two men walked a few more meters into the tunnel forged by the massive mining machine. The robot miners locked on to them, as expected. All four of them turned featureless faces in their direction. One of the robots scampered towards them. It pulled up in front of them, blocking their way.

"You are not authorized to be here," the mechanical miner said. A thin film of dust covered almost every inch of its composite carbon and gold alloy skin.

"Don't get excited. I'm calling base for authorization."

The robot regarded him with expressionless eyes. Logan switched his comm link to a direct, secured channel. An upgrade in the Communications Array now enabled high quality communication to base from the bottom of the deep Siloe Patera crater.

"Hi, Oscar. I'm at the north face site. I need clearance to take readings and gather some samples."

"Why didn't you bother to send me a formal request before leaving the base?"

"Because you haven't been overly cooperative with my requests."

"I'm going to report you for breach of procedure."

"Feel free. We're trying to complete our work here. I'm filling in for Corporal Blackstone because she's not physically able to leave the base due to her injury. If you refuse to let us do our work, I'll report *you* and your entire team for obstructing our audit. Would you like me to do that?"

"I'll transmit the clearance codes to the robots. Take your readings. Gather your samples, and then *please* leave quickly and let us get on with *our* work. We're trying to keep the Earth green, not fight with you and your team."

"Thanks. I'll keep that in mind."

"Oh, and please stay out of the restricted area. Behind those doors, we refine and accumulate finished product in temperature-controlled rooms for shipment back home. We don't want untrained amateurs messing up our delicate and precise process."

Logan ignored the insult. "C'mon, Rashawn. Let's do this."

Logan switched on the miniaturized camera mounted on the side of his space helmet.

"Are you getting this, Kate?"

"Loud and clear, Commander."

Logan approached the robot standing at a control panel near the big mining machine. As he drew closer to the giant ore processor, the sounds it made became deafening. The bright lights in the tunnel caused Logan and Rashawn to cast long shadows. The noise and the lighting made Logan feel uncomfortable.

"I need you to shut down the machine, Kaminsky."

"For how long?" Kaminsky came back.

"I don't know. I'm an amateur."

Through his comm link, he heard Kaminsky curse before he issued a command.

The robot's fingers played over the control panel. The ore processor backed away from the rock face on its haunch-like treads. The internal machinery wound down in a symphony of whirring, clicking, grinding, and groaning sounds.

"Shutdown sequence complete," the robot announced in a dispassionate voice.

Logan and Rashawn proceeded to take readings and gather samples from the rock face under Kate's watchful eye. The watchful eyes belonged not only to Kate: the robots monitored their every move. Logan felt their presence more as guards than observers.

The work went smoothly. Rashawn proved to be an able geological assistant. Kate had schooled them both. Logan would have taken more people down if he had them. Normally, no one traveled to the belly of Siloe Patera with only one partner. For safety, standard procedure called for a four-person team. Logan wasn't worried about accidents. He worried about the number of nosey robots surrounding him.

The next order of business promised to be harder to pull off than the sampling process.

"The WEC sent you a request to allow us into the storage area."

"I denied it," Kaminsky replied. "I've notified the WEC that we can't risk losing atmosphere while we're in the middle of packing the fuel rods. We could lose the entire shipment."

"You're concerned about airlock failure?"

"It can happen. And our refining process is proprietary. It's none of your business."

"I get the feeling you're hiding something."

"You have no right to go in there. Our job is to deliver the ore in excellent condition. We're doing that. We haven't received any complaints. There's no reason for you to enter the restricted area. You've completed your work here. Now get out of the mine."

The four robots moved towards them.

Rashawn drew his weapon. "They're comin' for us."

"Give it a few beats. Let's see if they head off towards the rooms."

The robots continued to close on them.

"What are you doing, Kaminsky?"

No response. Static.

"Take out the nearest one," Logan said.

Rashawn fired three bursts from his powerful laser pistol. The energy bolts severed the lead robot's torso in half. The top half clattered to the ground and exploded in a shower of sparks.

"Stop shooting," Kaminsky shouted. "Why are you firing on the miners?"

"We didn't hear from you. Your robots came at us."

"There was atmospheric interference. I lost you for a second. The robots are moving into position to lock down for the day. Now that you've destroyed one of them, I'll have to take our entire security system offline to open the outer doors."

Logan noticed the huge steel doors at the entrance of the mine opened and closed on semi-circular tracks. To the right of the doors, a control panel regulated ingress and egress.

"At least let us look in through the airlock porthole."

Logan waited a full minute for the response. "Suit yourself," Kaminsky said. "Make it quick."

The robots regrouped. One of them accompanied Logan and Rashawn to the restricted area. As they drew closer, it appeared the area consisted of four distinct sections. The section nearest them served as an airlock with a wide portal cut into the top half of the metal door. Through the portal, they observed a square stack of v-shaped ingots packed with their triangular bases alternately pointing up and down so that the ingots fit together neatly to conserve space.

And then Logan glimpsed something behind the ingots.

"What the hell is that?" he heard Rashawn exclaim.

The objects resembled multi-form sculptures, although Logan judged them to be machines of some sort. A transparent glass or plastic cylinder mounted on a mass of thick cables embedded with rows of ruby-red hemispheres looked like a medical device. The function of the second machine was a mystery; a concave silver sphere with ten concentric circles tapering down into a central core filled with an undulating mass of thread-thin purple strings. The purple mass in the center made it look like the machine was breathing.

"I'll be god-damned," Rashawn muttered.

"Can you see through the porthole?" Logan asked Kate.

"My visual is getting blurry. The signal must be degrading because you're so far into the mine."

"Roger that." *I can't wait to hear what Kate thinks of this when she sees it on the video recording. What will the WEC think when they see it in our report?*

"Let's get back to base," Logan said.

Their robot escort kept pace with them as they headed back to the tunnel entrance. The other two robots waited for them in front of the massive steel doors.

Logan couldn't shake the feeling of being a prisoner accompanied by a hostile security guard. *I'll feel better when we get back to base,* he thought. Then he wondered how much safer they would be there, after what they had just seen.

# Chapter 22

# MARS—ALIEN SHIP

SILENNA AND HER remaining crew members quickly discovered that a few of the ship's systems had been mysteriously compromised during the long journey to Mars. Because the design of their vessel included more redundant systems than previous models, the crew had escaped a crash landing. Their ship was simply a bigger, better version than the vessels that had carried the crews from the first mission to their deaths.

The crew now understood there was one glaring exception in the ship's design. No one had thought to back up the caretaker robot because no such robot had ever gone rogue before. This design oversight had nearly doomed the second mission.

After careful analysis, Arcon had arrived at the cause of the problems. Silenna, Elora and Galatar gathered in a small office on the ship's mezzanine level, waiting for the report. Diagrams of the faulty systems appeared on a screen in front of them.

"I've traced the source of the system failures back to the fuel system," Arcon informed them telepathically. "Before our interstellar missions to this planet, we had only used the new fuel for travel to the planets in our solar system. The variable of the new fuel being *used for the first time on an interstellar mission brought the system to my attention for investigation.*

*"My tests have revealed subtle alterations in the atomic structures of the fuel rods. These changes have been caused by prolonged exposure to cosmic radiation in the reactor core. The cosmic radiation caused the fuel to emit an energy signature which eventually penetrated the reactor shields and interfered with the stasis life support system, guidance and oxygenation systems, the care- taker robot, and a few other non-essential systems.*

*"The backup systems saved the ship from catastrophic failure. The fuel stored separately in the hold has not been affected."*

*"Our tests revealed slight anomalies in your sub-routines,"* Silenna told Arcon.

*"I am not aware of any anomalies."*

*"It explains your failure to neutralize the caretaker unit and reawaken us. We have flushed the problem from your central core. You are back to functioning at peak efficiency."*

*"Are you blaming me for the deaths of the crew members?"*

*"What happened is not your fault. We did not anticipate the occurrence of cosmic radiation contamination. We are not omniscient. Neither are you, Arcon."*

Silenna turned her attention back to the crew. "We'll repair the ship, then proceed with our investigation of the first mission. The remains of the ships bear invaluable information. We must harvest it."

\* \* \*

Four Martian days passed. The Aneleyan crew worked long hours to repair their ship (named the Yarlonquis, after the highest mountain on Aneleya). With Arcon's tutelage and oversight, Dmitri and Jon Henderson provided an extra pair of hands. With the repairs almost complete, Arcon woke Silenna from a deep sleep in the middle of the night.

"*I'm sorry to awaken you from your rest, Captain.*"

"*I was having blissful dreams of my early childhood and first love, Arcon. Is it important?*"

"*There is an Earth man outside.*"

Clad only in gray undershorts and a sports bra, Silenna sat up and stretched on the side of a bed that automatically supported every bone, muscle, organ and fiber of her well-toned body. The bed worked on her body during sleep, helping it to recover from the exertion of the day.

"*What does he want?*"

Telepathic communication came so naturally, she reflected, but the Aneleyans had chosen not to develop telepathic powers to converse. Using language was like using a muscle. Without it, the vocal chords and full-bodied expression atrophied. The issue of privacy also posed a problem.

"*He is banging on the main airlock. It appears he wants to come aboard.*"

Silenna considered the situation. If Arcon's ability to read minds stretched outside of the ship, her decision would have been easy. Well, she would know what the Earthling wanted soon enough.

"*Awaken the others and tell them to meet me below. Then open the airlock.*"

* * *

Surrounded by a riot of colored lights, Oscar Kaminsky held his breath as the lift propelled him upward through the floor of the giant ship. He found himself deposited in the middle of a white floor, surrounded by multi-colored structures that looked like storage bins. Interspersed among the rows of bins, he noticed circular work stations. The occasional oblong panel, angled at forty-five degrees and supported by a curved post, reminded him of giant lily pads on stems.

Jutting from the hull walls near the top of the ship, curved balconies circled the room underneath a ceiling that looked roughly twenty meters high. He imagined the balconies gave way to sleeping quarters or offices built out from the hull walls. He wondered why there was so much wasted space overhead. The colors, the silence, and the graceful architecture mixed with the sculpted soft lines of the electronics left him speechless.

His fear of the unknown and the creatures he might find aboard the alien vessel gave way to a sense of something more benign. The ship's interior engendered a welcoming feeling. He felt energized, and his mood brightened. A voice entered his head, startling him.

*"My name is Arcon. I am the ship's artificial intelligence. I will be acting as an interpreter for you and the crew members. I'm sure you have many questions, but first I must ask why you are here?"*

"I'm here to find out what happened to two of my men who came aboard your ship."

*"I will let you speak with our Captain. She is waiting for you in the cluster of work stations ten meters ahead."*

As he walked towards the circular complex, Kaminsky noticed a circle of what looked like stasis pods. Three of the pods had opened. The others remained closed and pitch black.

"How did you learn my language?"

*"I have the ability to master languages by scanning an alien subject. Please feel free to communicate with me telepathically. It will be easier for you."*

*Incredible,* Kaminsky thought.

With some trepidation, Kaminsky approached the circle of work stations. Entering, he found two gorgeous women and a blond, fair-skinned man with purple eyes waiting for him. He blinked. Each one of them stood seven or eight feet tall.

One of the women approached him. She had an athletic body with proportions shapely enough for a holographic magazine cover.

Her voice entered his mind. *"I am Silenna, Captain of the Yarlonquis. And you are?"*

Kaminsky found himself unable to respond. He stood there, taking in the sight of her.

"*Relax and think your response,*" Arcon prompted.

"*My name is Oscar Kaminsky. I am the Operations Manager of the Martian Mining Interplanetary colony.*"

"*What can I do for you, Mr. Kaminsky?*"

"*Two of my men are missing. I believe they are here on your ship.*"

"*What makes you think they are here?*"

"*I sent one of them here to bring back another man who disobeyed my orders.*"

Kaminsky saw Dmitri Semerov uncover from behind the far corner of the first row of storage bins.

"You don't have to lie for me, Silenna," Semerov said.

Kaminsky saw a hand grab Semerov by the arm and try to pull him back behind the bins. Semerov shook free from the hand and walked farther out into the open.

"What the fuck are you doing?" A voice from behind the bins—it had to belong to Jon Henderson.

"You're coming back to base with me, Dmitri." Kaminsky raised his voice. "You, too, Jon."

Henderson stepped out into the open. "I'm not going anywhere with you, Kaminsky. You can kiss my ass."

"That pretty much sums up my feelings too," Semerov said.

Oscar jettisoned the nice guy act. "*Look, Silenna, I don't know why you came to Mars, but let's get something straight. We came here first. We have every right to conduct our business here without any interference from you or your crew. These two men report to me. They have responsibilities to the company per the contracts they signed. I want them back.*"

The other two aliens stepped forward into flanking positions behind Silenna.

"*We have no intention of interfering in your business,*" Silenna said. "*As to your men, whatever they decide to do is up to them. I feel no obligation to either shelter them or turn them over to you. We came here to recover the remains of three of our ships that crashed here. The ship has learned from scanning your mind that you have*" *these remains in your possession. You are obliged to give back what is rightfully ours."*

Kaminsky strained to control his thoughts and emotions. The aliens scared him. At the same time, he wanted to decapitate Henderson and Semerov for disobeying orders.

*The remains of the ships are our property. They crashed. We found them. Now they belong to us. None of your crew members survived. That's the short and the long of it, as we say. You can go home and tell your superiors what happened."*

Silenna glared at him. He suddenly regretted speaking so bluntly to someone as physically imposing as the alien captain.

*"It would be wise to reconsider your position, Silenna told him evenly. "Leave the ship now, before I lose my patience with you."*

Adopting a baleful expression, Kaminsky called to Henderson and Semerov; "Do you guys really want to give up fifty million each to stay here?"

"I'm staying here," Dmitri called back.

"Me too," Henderson agreed.

"You'll go to jail if you breach your contracts," Kaminsky said.

"We'll go straight to hell if we don't breach them," Henderson shot back.

Kaminsky scowled at the men who no longer wanted to be his men. "You can't hide here."

He turned back to Silenna. *"How do I get out of here?"*

\* \* \*

Later, in the Communications Array, Kaminsky spoke with Benjamin Caliphas via secure laser link.

"This should never have happened," Caliphas said. "I depend on you to keep your staff in line."

"Semerov took matters into his own hands before I had a chance to speak to him. I never expected him to go rogue on us. His record is spotless. He's never been a troublemaker."

"I'd call three uncooperative aliens and two insubordinate workers trouble."

"I sent Henderson out to that ship to *kill* Dmitri, for God's sake. I didn't think Jon would lose his nerve. He's a greedy bastard."

"What do you propose we do now?"

"I'll negotiate with the aliens. They don't want to get in our way. We'll work something out. There's one more thing."

"Please make it a good thing."

"I stopped Marchant and his pilot from accessing the storage rooms. But I had to give them a peek through the door lock porthole. They may have seen something."

"If we're forced to let Marchant and his people into the storage rooms, I'll let you know how to handle it. Until you hear from me again, it's business as usual."

Caliphas severed the link. The screen faded to black.

# Chapter 23

# MARS—MINING BASE

THEY MET IN Kaneko's office. Logan noticed Kaneko's expression change from cheerful to serious when he activated the door lock.

"Something is wrong?" she inquired.

"Something is definitely not right," Kate replied.

Kaneko invited them to be seated.

Logan, Kate and Rashawn each pulled up one of the simple ergonomic chairs Kaneko had designed.

"It's time for full disclosure," Logan said. He glanced at Kaneko. "Each of us has to share what he or she knows before we decide what to do next. After this meeting, each of you will basically know too much. It means we'll all be in danger. We'll have to consider our next moves carefully. Why don't you get the ball rolling, Kate?"

Kate reviewed the notes on her tablet. Sweeping a stray hair away from her face, she began her report:

"The samples Logan and Rashawn gathered from the north face mine show low concentrations of Micromium ore. The readings Logan and I took at the strip mine also indicate low ore concentrations."

"If the two veins are nearly depleted, why is the corporation keeping it a secret?" Kaneko reflected.

"They might be milking their contract until they can find more ore," Kate offered. "They only get paid while the ore vein lasts. They can earn a big bonus if they strike more ore."

Rashawn shook his head and chuckled. Kaneko stared back at them, stone faced.

Logan turned to Rashawn. "You find this funny?"

"No, sir. I can't say as I'm surprised, though. I wouldn't put anything past these miners."

"Tell Kate and Kaneko what you saw in the storage room."

"We saw two machines. I've never seen anything like them before."

"Your discoveries are intriguing," Kaneko said evenly. "What I've discovered is equally interesting. I carbon dated the cell samples I found at the strip mine. Since reporting the results to Logan, I re-tested to verify the data." She inhaled deeply. "The cells aren't millions or even hundreds of years old. They are less than three decades old."

Shaking his head again, Rashawn leaned back in his chair. "Kaminsky wouldn't let us into the rooms. He said we might disturb the atmosphere inside while they were packing a shipment. It sounded fishy to me and Logan."

"There's something else," Logan said. "Rashawn and I thought the robots were attacking us for a minute there in the mine. After Rashawn blew up one of them, Kaminsky couldn't wait to get us out of there."

Logan noticed Kate's face blanch visibly in response to his report of the incident. Their eyes met. Instinct pulled at him to reassure her. It hurt to beat down the impulse and the darkness from the empty place inside him.

"How did Kaminsky explain the behavior of the robots?" Kaneko asked. Logan detected an edge of fear creeping into her normally calm voice.

"He said the robots were simply moving in formation to close up shop for the day."

"Do you believe him?"

"Nope," Rashawn interjected.

A moment of silence settled over the group, after which Logan spoke.

"I think it's time to make a preliminary report to the WEC. We'll ask them to get a high court ruling compelling the corporation to let us into those storage rooms. It's clearly in the public interest."

"And whatever we find in there should answer at least some of our questions." Kaneko added.

Logan eyed the three of them. "Are we agreed?"

Kate, Rashawn and Kaneko exchanged looks. Rashawn agreed with a thumbs-up. Kaneko nodded her assent. "Makes sense," Kate said.

\* \* \*

Kaminsky sat in the head near his work station taking a much-needed crap when he heard the security-alarms go off. *I finally find the time to take a dump,* he thought, *and the fucking world is coming to an end.*

As he rushed to clean himself up, he heard Derek Carpenter, his senior software engineer, saying, "Something's out there."

Pulling up his pants, Kaminsky rushed out of the tiny bathroom into the middle of the Operations Array. Through the panoramic window behind his desk, he observed something that nearly made him finish his interrupted crap in his pants. The vessel slipped between two of the white poles mounted with security cameras that ringed the complex of domes and interconnecting tunnels comprising the mining base.

The sleek body and boomerang wings of the vehicle mimicked the alien ship Semerov and Henderson had discovered in the uncharted crater. As it drew closer, hovering about three meters off the ground, he thought: *it must be some sort of a shuttle craft. The goddamned aliens have come to pay us a visit. They're here to either blow us off the planet or talk. Breathe. Don't panic.*

"Let's stay calm," Kaminsky told Carpenter and his assistant, Paul Blömfeld, a Swede with blood as cold as his native country in the winter. "I'm ninety-nine percent sure that ship belongs to the one we found in the crater."

"If the babes inside are as good-looking as you say they are, I can't wait to meet them."

"You may be a stud, Carpenter, but I think you'll find these babes more than you can handle."

He watched the shuttle sprout two tripods from underneath the front and rear of the fuselage. It landed about thirty meters away from the dome. A porthole opened and a set of steps unfolded to the ground. Moments later, two aliens exited the craft wearing streamlined spacesuits colored in dazzling yellow accented with black helmets and boots.

"Man, they're tall," Blömfeld said.

"They could break you in half like a twig."

"So, they're here to give us a hard time?" Carpenter said.

"I came on pretty strong on their ship. It didn't seem to rattle them. I think they're here to talk," Kaminsky said. *One thing's for sure: they're not here to fuck our brains out.*

"The one in front is signaling like he wants in," Blömfeld said.

"It's probably a she," Kaminsky said. "Open the outer lock for them."

Ten minutes later, the two aliens entered the Operations Array. Their boots made squeaking sounds on the hard floor. The one in the rear held up a device that looked like a silver pencil. Kaminsky held up a hand to keep his people calm. He guessed the alien was testing the air quality. The one behind tapped the one in front, and both visitors removed their space helmets. Kaminsky recognized Silenna and the other woman from the ship. He introduced Silenna to his men. Carpenter and Blömfeld stared unabashedly at the Amazonian aliens. The domed ceiling accommodated their height, but Kaminsky figured it still must have been an uncomfortable squeeze through the short corridor of the airlock.

Kaminsky watched Silenna unclip a black circular device from her utility belt. She held the device in both hands as if it were an offering.

Kaminsky heard a voice in his head say: *"This will help us to communicate. It is a portable version of the translation program we used on the ship."*

Kaminsky invited Silenna and her companion to follow him into the recreation room after making an announcement to clear all personnel from the area. He told Carpenter and Blömfeld to get back to work and keep their mouths shut regarding the presence of their visitors.

He led the aliens through the tunnel to the recreation room. Holding their space helmets, they bent uncomfortably until they reached the open space.

Once inside the room, Kaminsky tried to make the women comfortable. They sat awkwardly on a sofa against the wall with their knees shooting up in the air.

*"I think the floor will work better,"* Kaminsky offered.

Silenna introduced Elora. They bent awkwardly to the floor and sat cross-legged, leaning against the sofa for support. The translation device lay on a coffee table in front of them. Kaminsky pulled up a chair and sat. The aliens looked considerably more comfortable, although he imagined they would feel even better without their boots on. *Let them feel at least some discomfort. Did they hear that?* He couldn't hear them thinking. Could they hear his thoughts, and could he hear only the thoughts they wanted him to hear?

The woman's voice came to him: *"I think you know why we're here."*

*"Let me guess. You want access to the remains of your ships."*

*"Exactly."*

Kaminsky immediately regretted boarding the ship in a fruitless effort to retrieve the worthless traitors Semerov and Henderson. *"Can you read my mind?"*

*"No. The translation device can pick up your thoughts, but it only sends the ones you want us to hear. If the translator relayed all thoughts, then our communication would be jumbled, almost like static. There is also a need for confidentiality in most exchanges, especially business negotiations and diplomatic discussions. The device is quite practical."*

Kaminsky sat quietly for a moment, enthralled by the wondrous alien technology and the alluring beauty of the two women. Then he came back to Earth, or Mars, as it were. *"There isn't much left of your first mission."*

Silenna's companion spoke up; the one with the piercing brown eyes, porcelain skin, and lustrous red hair cascading in curls down to her shoulders. *"We are having difficulty understanding your claim that our ships belong to you."*

Kaminsky laughed. *"We have a saying on our home world: possession is nine tenths of the law. Do you understand what I mean?"*

Silenna sat up straighter and shook her russet mane of hair. She pulled it back into flowing tresses with her long fingers. For a second, Kaminsky wished he were three feet taller. This woman exuded confidence, strength, and sexuality without trying.

*"I understand you, Mr. Kaminsky. Do you understand that our advanced technology puts you at an unfortunate disadvantage if we can't come to an agreement? Let's stop wasting time. What is your decision?"*

She was right, of course. He knew when he invited them in where the discussion would end up. He simply couldn't resist playing the game. He never went down without a fight.

*"I'll give you what you want under one condition."*

*"State it."*

*"Take what's left of your ships. Do whatever you want with it. All we ask in return is a translated download with complete information about your ship's artificial intelligence and propulsion systems."*

*"You ask too much, Mr. Kaminsky."*

Silenna turned to her partner. They spoke in tones rather than words. Their language sounded more like abstract jazz than speech. When they finished, she turned back to him. *"You can keep the remains of our ships after we examine them. That is my final offer."*

Kaminsky could barely contain his glee. *"I suppose that's fair. You have a deal."*

*"What does 'a deal' mean?"*

"*It means we have an agreement. I want it in writing.*"

"*In your language or ours?*"

"*In our language, assuming your smartass ship can write in English.*"

"*What does 'smartass' mean?*"

"*Never mind.*"

Silenna looked at him with a stern expression. "*I give you my word, Mr. Kaminsky. You don't need a piece of paper. Do I have yours?*"

Oscar hesitated. He decided not to push his luck. "*All right. You have my word. One hundred percent.*"

# Chapter 24

# MARS—NORTH FACE MINE

FLANKED BY RASHAWN and Kate, Logan approached the yawning entrance of the north face mine. Kaminsky had no choice except to allow them entrance into the storage rooms after the Supreme Court passed a resolution compelling the mining corporation to comply with the audit team's request.

The timing turned out to be perfect. A day before the mission, Kaneko declared Kate fit for outside duties after conducting a thorough examination.

The stark play of light and shadow coupled with the sight of the brutish mining machine gave Logan the creeps. His curiosity to finally explore the mystery-shrouded storage rooms easily offset his unsettling feelings. Kate and Rashawn's banter during the long decent into the deep crater indicated to Logan they shared his enthusiasm for the mission.

As they entered the cavern through the thick outer doors, Logan saw flashlight beams dancing on the ceiling and walls.

Three mining robots came out of the gloom towards them.

"I can't see any reason why Kaminsky would order robots with flashlights into the mine," Logan said to Kate and Rashawn through his comm link. "Their eyes are designed to adapt to the varying light in here."

Logan reached out to hold Kate back, but she kept walking deeper into the mine. He watched the robots peel off and take up strategic positions against the cavern wall. Despite their less-than-intimidating stature, they made his flesh crawl. Then he noticed something more unnerving: the menacing robots held no flashlights.

Drawing their energy weapons, Logan and Rashawn joined Kate. Her flashlight beam illuminated a space-suited body near the storage room door lock. Another flashlight beam flashed back in their faces, temporarily blinding them.

"There are two of them," Kate announced after pointing her flashlight back into the dim light. Her beam revealed arms and legs and space helmets colored in yellow and black.

"Those aren't the corporate colors of the mining staff," Rashawn pointed out.

"Let's find out who they are," Logan said. "Move slowly and point your weapons at the ground, but stay frosty."

Kate stepped behind Logan as they made their way cautiously into the ghostly gloom. *Good move,* Logan thought. Kate's burden of sensitive measuring equipment and geological tools left no tolerance for a conventional weapon in her utility belt.

Logan thought he heard a faint voice in his head. It startled him. Rashawn suddenly came to a halt. Kate grabbed him by the arm from behind. He heard the voice distinctly now.

*"You gave your word. Why have you come bearing weapons?"*

"Are you hearing a voice or am I experiencing oxygen deprivation symptoms?" Logan asked his comrades.

Rashawn nodded. "It's in my head."

Kate came forward beside him. "Those people up ahead are talking to us telepathically."

*"Who are you?"* Logan thought.

*"Come forward. Keep your weapons down,"* came the reply. It sounded like a woman's voice; confident and unafraid. She spoke in perfect English with no discernible accent.

"Stay behind me," Logan told Rashawn. "Kate, you stay behind Rashawn."

They moved ahead single file.

Logan's flashlight played over the figures standing in front of the storage rooms.

"Will you look at the size of them," he said as they came within ten meters of the storage area. He motioned for Rashawn and Kate to hold their ground with him.

They stood there observing the tall, space-suited figures.

Logan turned in time to see the three mining robots pulling up ominously behind them, five meters back.

He turned back to Kate. Her attention remained riveted ahead. "They look human, except for their size."

"I think we've made first contact with Martians," Rashawn said.

*"Why have you come here with weapons?"* The woman's voice again; repeating the question.

Rashawn said it the moment Logan thought it. "They think we're from the corporation."

Logan handed his weapon to Rashawn. "Stay here and cover me."

He moved forward with his hands open and his arms in the air. *"We are not with the miners. We're here to observe the mining operation and report our findings to an independent organization back on Earth."*

Stopping ten feet in front of the two giants, Logan noticed one of them holding a black disc in one hand. As he stood there ready for anything, the woman spoke. It seemed like her voice sprouted from the middle of his brain.

*"The disc is a translation device. It allows us to communicate this way."*

A shiny silver faceplate prevented him from seeing the faces of the two giants. Did they come from another planet or did they live in majestic cities underneath the surface?

*"Are you from here or somewhere else?"*

*"We are not from this world. Three of our ships crash-landed here some time ago."* The one nearest him gestured toward the airlock. *"These storage rooms hold the remains of our ships."*

*Beings from another planet. Corporate shenanigans. What next?* Logan's mind swam. He forced himself to regain control of his thoughts. He pointed to the airlock. *"To complete our work, we need to go in there."*

The giants nodded their understanding in unison.

His mind swarmed with questions. How did these aliens know the remains of their ships rested inside the storage rooms? Did they intend to go inside? Without the codes, how did they intend to get in? Did they have clearance?

*"Does the mining colony know you are here?"*

This time he heard a male voice speaking in an unusual lilting tone. *"Yes."*

*So, the corporation knows about these aliens, yet it made no mention of them to anyone back home,* Logan thought. *I'm going to have a long talk with Kaminsky when we get back to base.*

*"I believe we can help each other if we work together,"* Logan offered.

He heard the woman's voice again. *"How can you help us?"*

A fair question. *"I believe we're on the same side. The governments of Earth have vital interests here. It seems you have important business here, too. We can help you get what you came for. You'll need our support to avoid misunderstandings with our terrestrial authorities."*

The aliens turned to each other, gesturing, probably conversing in their alien tongue via a secure comm link. They turned back to him and the woman spoke.

*"Your offer is accepted. I am Silenna. My companion is Galatar."*

Logan called to Kate and Rashawn to join him. He introduced himself and his team to the two space travelers, briefly outlining their functions. With the formalities out of the way, it was time to enter the storage rooms. Logan watched the one named Galatar enter a code into an interface near the door. He motioned for the aliens to proceed into the rooms. He thought: *"I have the entry code. We'll follow you in."*

Bending to avoid the top of the door frame, Silenna and Galatar entered the airlock. Logan imagined their discomfort in the cramped quarters while they waited for the atmosphere inside to normalize. When the cycle completed, Logan entered the code Kaminsky had given him. He entered the outer door, followed by Kate and Rashawn. When the pressure and oxygen levels reached optimal readings, the interior door gave way to a room stacked full of ore. He estimated the ceiling of the room at about eight meters high.

Placed neatly together, the V-shaped ore ingots lined two of the walls. Square stacks of the ingots sat in rows on the floor with aisles in between to allow for movement. The ingots appeared larger than Logan expected. Their characteristic quartz-like veins glistened under the bright LED lighting.

"Leave your helmets on," Logan told Kate and Rashawn. "The air should be breathable, but I'd rather stay on the safe side."

The aliens had already begun examining the exotic machines stored against the wall on his left. The conveyor belt stretching through the center of the room and laden with ore ingots captured Logan's attention next. The conveyor belt fed the ingots into a chute with grinding gears visible through vents in the side. Although Kaminsky had shut down the line, the process looked simple enough to deduce. The grinding machine broke the ingots down into powder and injected it into a pipe that fed into the wall separating the second storage room from the one they occupied. In the second room, he supposed, the powdered ore went through a series of machines to check for previously undetected impurities. The machines then formed the purified product into fuel pellets suitable for the fusion reactors back on Earth.

Kate and Rashawn broke away to snap pictures of everything in the room for their reports. Ample lighting from circular lights embedded in the ceiling made their job easier, although five space-suited beings working in a jam-packed room with narrow aisles and measuring ten meters wide by thirty meters long made movement challenging. The off-white porcelain walls bare of ingots made Logan feel like he was inside a fifty-year-old GE refrigerator.

Logan couldn't resist joining the giant aliens. The two machines shaped in concave concentric circles with undulating threads in the center interested him more than anything else in the room. The aliens pressed buttons on the rims of both machines, causing the concentric circles to change colors, mostly in the pastel range.

*"Can I ask you what those machines do?"*

Silenna answered. *"These are navigation computers from the wings of one of the two smaller ships. Both computers are malfunctioning. Our ships are designed with these devices in the wings and fuselage. We depend on them to fly our ships and plot courses. We may have already found the primary cause for the crashes."*

Silenna and Galatar abruptly rose from their kneeling positions alongside the navigation computers.

*"Excuse us. We must measure the emissions from the fuel in here."*

*"What fuel?"*

Silenna pointed to a nearby stack of ingots. *"The fuel from our ships."*

## Chapter 25

# MARS—STORAGE ROOMS

THE LIGHTS IN the storage room seemed to shine brighter for a few seconds. Logan chalked the phenomenon up to his imagination and the shock of what Silenna had just revealed.

*I should be making notes on everything in here.* Instead, he watched the aliens take readings with devices resembling silver dollars from the stacks of ore spread throughout the room. Whatever their findings, it seemed to be of great interest to them, judging by their head movements and gestures when they communicated. His mind raced with one unanswered question after another. Kate glanced back at him, probably wondering why he stood idly while they furiously inputted notes of their observations. He let them go about their business for the time being.

While he waited for Silenna and Galatar to finish their tasks, he made notes describing them and every detail he remembered from their conversations. Every sentence he wrote spawned another question. When it appeared the two giants had finished their work, Logan called Kate and Rashawn to join him. They objected, wondering what was so important that it had to interfere with their work. It took a direct order to get them to stop what they were doing.

After re-uniting with Kate and Rashawn, Logan led them through the stacks of ore until they reached Silenna and Galatar. He found them in what appeared to be a deep conversation. Breaking off their conversation, they turned towards him.

*"I'm sorry. I didn't mean to interrupt. Do you mind if I ask a few more questions?"*

*"What is "do you mind?"*

*"Is it okay, or uhmm, more like: is it acceptable to you?"*

*"It is okay,"* Silenna replied.

*"Thank you."* He picked up the nearest ingot. It weighed less in his hand than it appeared in mass.

*"These are from your ship?"*

Silenna nodded.

*"Is it natural or manufactured?"*

*"It comes from an ore found on our two moons. What you are holding is a highly enriched version of the natural ore."*

Holding the ingot in both hands, Logan extended it towards Kate and Rashawn. He had the honor of stating the obvious.

"The corporation is exporting alien rocket fuel back to Earth. Micromium is not indigenous to Mars. This means the supply is limited to the alien ships that crashed here."

"It explains the low readings I took from the mines," Kate said through her comm link. "MMI must have planted ore in the ground at the mining sites to simulate a mining operation, but it's a fake."

Logan put the ingot aside. His mind raced. What had they stumbled into? Would his WEC superiors believe this? *Okay, calm down. Your job is to gather information and report.*

*"How many are in your crew?"*

*"There are only three of us left from an original crew of eight. Our deep-sleep life support systems malfunctioned. One of the miners working for the corporation saved our lives."*

*"Who saved you?"*

*"The one named Dmitri Semerov."*

Logan made a mental note of the name. He removed his helmet. *"Can you breathe in this atmosphere?"*

In response, the aliens removed their helmets. Their humanoid features surprised Logan. Silenna's piercing green eyes stared at him out of a face chiseled with character lines and features lovely enough to stop traffic at rush hour. The one named Galatar had an altogether different effect on him. With his purple eyes, white complexion, and curly blond hair the color of spun gold, the man had the look of a stage actor in a surrealist play.

*"Since you are using this fuel on your home world, I must tell you that some of it has been contaminated by exposure to cosmic radiation. It will likely cause machinery failure,"* Galatar said.

*"How do you know this?"*

*"From the tests we just made. We also know that contaminated fuel damaged systems on our ship. We assume it caused the guidance systems to fail on the ships we originally sent here. The pilots must have relied on false data from their guidance systems which caused the ships to crash."*

More bad news for the WEC to digest. Kate and Rashawn punched notes into their hand-held computers. Later, they would organize the videos, photos, and notes they took to produce their reports.

Kate pointed to the cylindrical machine. Silenna told them the machine healed diseases and wounds. Silenna's explanation confirmed what Logan had surmised when he first laid eyes on the contraption. Logan wanted to ask more questions, but his instincts told him it was time to stop jawing and move on to the other rooms. Kaminsky had a short fuse. He anticipated that they barely had enough time remaining to adequately cover the other rooms.

*"Are you ready to go next door?"*

Silenna gestured for him to lead the way. They found the door into the next compartment. Logan entered the combination Kaminsky had given him. The aliens squeezed through after them. In the second room, they again found ore ingots stacked high to the top of two walls. Logan now knew why the miners had loaded the rooms with ore—this was all there was on the entire planet.

In the center of the room, the pipe from the wall connecting to the first room led into three machines. He imagined the first one purified the powdered ore, the second one measured the ore, and the third machine baked the powder into cookie-sized pellets for the fusion reactors. Rashawn and Kate began taking videos and making notes of the process.

Looking up from the production line, he followed Silenna and Galatar's gaze. Eight pods lay stacked in two columns against the wall facing them. The pods looked like large coffins made of black, shiny glass. More alien machinery plundered from the ship lay piled on shelves drilled into the wall next to the pods.

Galatar and Silenna walked to the pods. With the same silver-dollar-like monitoring devices they used to test the fuel, the aliens slowly scanned each pod.

"*What are you looking for?*" Logan asked them.

"*These sleep pods came from the mother ship,*" Galatar replied. "*We're looking for survivors.*"

Silenna froze as she passed her device over the pod at the top of one column. They stood facing one another after completing their scans. Galatar said something aloud to Silenna in their native language and she responded. It sounded to Logan like bass and high-pitched tones combining in both rhythmic and arrhythmic music.

Silenna turned and addressed the three of them. "*We found one survivor—the captain of the ship. We're going into the next chamber to see if there are more pods.*"

As Silenna and Galatar moved away from the pods, Logan saw something that almost made his heart stop. A white boot peaked out from behind a pod lying in a corner of the room. Walking to the pod, Logan pulled a spacesuit from behind the pod. Another suit lay beneath it. He bent over the pod to retrieve the other suit. As Kate and Rashawn joined him, he spread both suits face down on the floor. Reading the names on the back of the suits made him want to scream. The suits belonged to Jesse MacMahn and Anna Petrovsky, the two mining colonists who had died in a meteor shower. He noticed the suits showed no visible tears. He remembered Kaminsky telling him the suits had been "recycled." What were they doing here?

*Oh, shit. There's only one reason they let us in here. Why didn't
I see it sooner?*

The lights went out in the room. They stood in total darkness for
a moment. Logan scrambled for his flashlight and turned it on. The
others did the same. Their beams painted the walls and ceilings and
reflected off each other.

"It must be a power failure," Kate said.

Other than putting on their helmets to protect them from the
freezing temperatures, the aliens seemed unperturbed by the blackout.
They found the door to the next room and pushed through it in search
of more survivors.

With the atmosphere in the room rapidly degrading, Logan and
the others slammed their helmets on. He didn't have to tell them what
to do next. They headed back through the doorway to the first room
and the exit.

"I sure as hell hope the airlock works," Rashawn said.

"It should be set up on an independent system in case the primary
power fails," Logan said. He didn't want to tell the others what he
was thinking.

They reached the airlock. The interface lit up at Logan's touch.
He entered the code to open the lock. A message in red letters flashed
at the top of the panel: ACCESS DENIED.

"Oh, shit." Rashawn said.

"Call Kaminsky," Kate said.

"He's not going to help us," Logan said. "They had no intention
of letting us out. We've seen too much."

\* \* \*

Oscar Kaminsky banged on the central strut of the alien ship. Behind
him stood three mining robots.

A large oval blur in the strut appeared.

*Open Sesame,* Kaminsky thought.

The passageway into the ship opened. Kaminsky stepped through the oval opening, followed by one of the robots. To his dismay, the hatch shut before his other two mechanical escorts stepped inside.

*I've just lost two thirds of my army.* Amid swirling colored lights, he felt the platform engage, pushing him and the lone robot up into the ship.

The alien named Elora stood alone in a barren space between the colorful storage bins and empty sleep pods. The lighting in the ship seemed more subdued than Kaminsky remembered from his first visit.

Elora made no attempt to move forward or greet them. Kaminsky decided to take the initiative and approach her. Elora raised an outstretched arm and an open hand. Her voice entered his head. *"Stay where you are."* Kaminsky obeyed the command. The robot shadowed his every move.

Elora approached them with long graceful strides. She wore white overalls resplendent with tools peeking out of pockets on her arms and legs. He noticed the handle of a shiny silver device strapped to her waist in what looked like a holster.

*I've worn out my welcome. Damn.*

Her voice again: *"I know why you've come. The AI system can read minds. Tell your staff to let my crew and the others out of the storage rooms. You will not leave this ship if you keep them locked up."*

Kaminsky removed his helmet. He tried to remain calm and friendly. He tried not to feel naked.

*"If you give us the information we want, we'll return Silenna and Galatar to you unharmed. It's a simple trade. We download the information from your computers into my friend the mining robot and everybody wins. We're not asking for much—the propulsion and AI systems. Silenna refused my request. I had no choice. I had to detain your crew to strengthen our bargaining position. Let's be done with this unpleasantness and do the trade."*

*"You've broken your word. Why should I believe you?"*

*"Like I said. I had no choice. You want what you want, but you refuse to give up anything in return. That's not the way business works in our part of the galaxy."*

*"I will not bargain with you."*

Stepping aside, Kaminsky turned to the robot. "Kill her."

The mining robot raised its hands and opened fire with laser bursts issuing from its palms and, a second later, from its eyes. Kaminsky expected to see Elora chopped to pieces in the searing fusillade.

Instead, Elora shot up into the vast open space below the unusually high ceiling. Landing on an overhanging balcony, she quickly disappeared behind the gentle curve of the guard barrier.

*Fuck. The bitch is wearing an anti-gravity belt.*

Before he could think of what to do next, Henderson and Semerov wheeled from behind opposite ends of the storage bins bearing energy weapons trained on the robot.

The robot reacted instantly. It discharged a barrage of suppressing fire. Semerov and Henderson took to the air before the shots landed.

*Those dick-heads are wearing the same damn belts.*

Soaring overhead, Henderson and Semerov fired at the robot while it jumped and jerked out of harm's way. Watching the two traitors try to avoid crashing into each other and the walls of the ship, Kaminsky concluded they had about as much chance of hitting a moving target as a bumble bee surviving in a cyclone. Sooner than later, his robot would decorate some part of the ship with their blood and bones.

His engineers had secretly installed a warfare mode in three of his robots as a precaution against unforeseen circumstances. Kaminsky had figured he might have to use it someday against his own men. He never imagined an unforeseen circumstance like this one. It was the first time he'd had to activate the warfare mode, aside from tests. His engineers had done a good job. They had made the miners into soldiers. Too bad the other two hadn't joined the party, but his lone soldier was more than holding its own.

While the robot continued to evade damage, Kaminsky sprinted to shelter in a work station out of the line of fire.

He watched from there as the battle raged. The robot fired an X pattern of shots at Henderson from its hands and eyes. The fusillade caught him flush in the chest. He hit the floor face down. Fingers of blood spread out in all directions from his mangled body. *One down, two to go.*

Elora spiraled down from the balcony with her pistol blazing. Her sudden appearance scared the crap out of him. He watched Semerov take a hit in the shoulder before the alien tigress tore the robot apart with a corkscrew of laser blasts. *Game over.*

Securing his helmet, Kaminsky scampered over to the opening in the floor leading to the exit tunnel. He gambled that Elora had neglected to close the opening in all the excitement. *Yes. It's open!* He dove over the edge. The platform whisked him down to ground level. The outer door opened automatically.

*Elora must be tending to Henderson and Semerov. She's not coming after me.* He fled to the rover, accompanied by his two 'bots. As he fired up the engine, he began considering how to explain the failed mission to his boss. The exercise promised to be harder than surviving the cluster-fuck aboard the alien vessel.

* * *

Back aboard ship, Dmitri kneeled next to what was left of Jon Henderson. He couldn't exactly call him a friend; not after what happened, but Henderson had risen to the occasion at crunch time. *Sorry you didn't make it, Hollywood. Happy trails, brother.*

Standing above him, Elora offered him a hand. *"Come, Dmitri. Let's get that shoulder of yours healed before you lose more blood. There's nothing we can do for Jon Henderson except give him a proper burial like the lost members of our crew. I promise you, these deaths will be avenged. Now we are at war."*

# Chapter 26

# MARS—STORAGE ROOMS

LOGAN, KATE, AND Rashawn surrounded the airlock in a semi-circle. They had spent the last twenty minutes trying different combinations and fiddling with the circuit board to open the exit with no luck. They took care not to damage the circuitry. Rendering it inoperative meant certain death. Blasting the door open with an energy weapon posed an even less desirable option. Igniting lingering pockets of oxygen tended to create explosive fireballs—not a recommended practice in the astronaut survival manual for escape from underground rooms.

"Any other evac ideas?" Logan asked.

The sounds of Silenna and Galatar struggling with something behind them interrupted the silence.

The front of a sleep pod upended on its side peeked through the door to the first storage room. A minute later, the two aliens emerged into the antechamber pushing the sleep pod. Silenna removed something from her utility belt that looked like a military canteen. Pressing a button on the top, she placed it on the ground and moved away from it. Metal rods shot from the spout of the canteen. The rods aligned themselves into a diamond shape resting a few feet above the floor. Thin wires sprouted from the rods and meshed into an odd-looking gurney. Galatar loaded the sleep pod onto it.

Logan exchanged astonished looks with Kate and Rashawn. For the aliens, carrying a fabrication template for a medical sled that deployed like an inflatable raft was just another routine occurrence in a long workday. Logan noticed the sled floated slightly above the floor, apparently supported by an anti-gravity feature. It made sense that the aliens had come prepared to transport machines or bodies from the crashed vessels back to their ship. And obviously, they had anticipated the possibility of finding survivors in the rooms. Astronauts, regardless of where they called home, needed the optimism gene to explore outer space. What were the odds against finding one of their own alive here? He hated to break the bad news.

*"We're locked in,"* Logan told the aliens. *"Kaminsky changed the digital combination to the exit. Do you have something that can get us out of here?"*

The aliens shook their heads.

Logan glanced at the oxygen read-out on the HUD inside his helmet. Less than thirty minutes of air left.

He tried calling Kaminsky again. "Oscar Kaminsky, this is Commander Marchant. Open these doors. Let's talk. You're only making this worse for yourself and your people."

Dead silence. Again. *Kaminsky must have one hell of a plan for covering up our deaths.*

An unfamiliar voice came from somewhere outside the room. *"I'm here. I'll open the door. Stand back."* Logan and the others looked at each other and then to the aliens.

*"We contacted our other surviving crew member when the lights went out,"* Silenna told them. *"Her name is Elora. She has the equipment to rescue us."*

*"Why didn't you tell us?"* Logan asked.

*"An oversight. We've been preoccupied with searching for more survivors."* She pointed to the sleep pod. *"The Captain is the only survivor of the three crews; one barely alive and twenty-three dead. We must get him back to the ship soon."*

After they had stepped back from the airlock, Silenna gave Elora the go-ahead to open it.

The airlock's interior door opened. Logan, Kate, and Rashawn went into the compression chamber first. Would the outer airlock work?

Seconds ticked by. Their lives hung in the balance.

The pressure gauges began moving. The atmosphere in the chamber normalized to the outside atmosphere. The outer door opened. They entered the cave.

The two aliens followed them through the lock, guiding the sled in front of them.

Logan had never seen a more welcome sight than the statuesque Elora waiting to greet them in her black helmet and yellow space suit. Her utility belt held myriad devices of different shapes and sizes. She clutched a y-shaped, shiny black tool in her right hand. It had to be the miracle working device she had used to decode the airlock security system. She had also come armed with double barrel silver cylinders holstered to her hips.

They walked towards the imposing metallic doors guarding the cave. Logan expected to encounter miner robots waiting for them. None appeared. Kaminsky had sent no backup. *The bastard never expected us to get out of the storage rooms.*

Rashawn asked Elora the obvious question: *"How did you get here so quickly?"*

*"We use a high-speed skiff to travel on planetary surfaces.* She gestured toward the mouth of the mine. *"It awaits us beyond those great doors. Will you come with us to our mother ship?"*

*"With great pleasure,"* Rashawn volunteered, without asking for permission from his commanding officer. Logan had no problem with the breach in protocol. Elora's presence was nothing short of a miracle.

Logan sensed the morale of the group building. They quickened their pace. He guessed Kate and Rashawn felt what he was feeling now: the sweet anticipation and curiosity of sweeping over the sands of Mars in a wondrous alien speed boat towards the mysterious mother ship. The child in him woke up. The heavy responsibility of the mission and their brush with death dissolved into a welcome sense of relief and sheer joy.

As they approached the ponderous doors, he heard gears grinding and saw the light beyond the mouth of the tunnel fading as the doors closed them inside.

*One thing you can say about Kaminsky,* Logan thought. *The son-of-a-bitch is persistent.*

Logan's suit spoke to him in its characteristic calming tone: "Warning: O2 level has reached fifteen percent. Replenish supply."

Kate touched his arm. Rashawn drew his weapon. Clearly, the idea of suffocating in the mine terrified all three of them.

*"The control panel is on the other side of the doors,"* Elora said. *"I can't open it from here."*

Rashawn looked over to Logan.

"Have at it," Logan said with a flourish.

Rashawn fired his laser in short bursts for several minutes until the weapon had discharged all of its energy. He succeeded only in opening a small hole about six inches in diameter in the door to their right.

Unless the aliens could reduce their bodies into energy streams and beam them through the hole, they were screwed.

Logan turned to the aliens — their only hope, at this point.

Motioning them to step back, Elora drew her silver weapons. The double-barrel cylinders spat four pencil-thin, pale blue beams at the doors. The beams slammed into the gray monoliths. Logan watched in awe as thousands of tiny cracks wormed their way out from the centers of both doors. In the ensuing ear-splitting explosion, a dense cloud of shimmering metallic shards flew into the tunnel and fluttered to the ground like dead butterflies.

Beyond the mouth of the tunnel, he caught his first glimpse of the skiff, a sleek craft with a boomerang wing and muscular engines mounted on the back end. The artificial lighting around it reflected its pearlescent yellow coloring. Its unusual shape surprised him. Under the circumstances, it looked as gorgeous as Silenna.

They stepped through the alien-made exit. Taking the lead in the tunnel, Silenna led them out to the floor of the crater. Behind them, Galatar pulled the sleep pod along on the anti-gravity sled. Ahead, half in shadow and half in the glare of the artificial lighting, the sleek ship with a boomerang wing waited to whisk them to safety.

Suddenly, two miner robots emerged out of the shadows.

Dropping the harness of the sled, Galatar ran towards the robots. They fired on the android with bursts from their palms and eyes. The salvos lit up the protective energy shield Galatar had deployed. Logan watched Galatar grab the lead robot, rip its head off, and fling it into the shadows. The other robot kept firing at point blank range. Galatar turned to attack it, but the machine-gun fusillade of energy bursts tore his shield apart. Logan watched helplessly as the energy barrage shattered Galatar's body into flaming fragments. Before the surviving robot turned its attention away from the carnage, Silenna pushed him and the others behind an outcropping of rocks to the left of the tunnel entrance.

From behind the rocks, Logan watched Elora, standing exposed in front of the tunnel, fire her awesome weapons. She calmly dismembered the deadly robot as if it were a cardboard target on a firing range.

Without a word, Silenna walked away to retrieve the sleep pod. Elora approached them.

"*We're so grateful for your help,*" Logan said. "*I'm very sorry for what happened to Galatar.*"

Kate and Rashawn added their condolences.

"*He sacrificed himself to distract the robots,*" she said, matter-of-factly.

With her weapons held at the ready and scanning the terrain in front of them in case of another ambush, Elora led them to the ship. As they approached the vessel, Logan noticed a glimmering energy field surrounding it and three rear-mounted engines. They looked powerful; maybe capable of producing enough thrust to boost the craft into orbit.

Elora pushed a button on her utility belt and the energy field dissolved. Stairs descended from under the forward strut. They boarded the vessel with Silenna bringing up the rear. After Logan and the others came safely aboard, Elora stood at the top of the stairs with a hand-held device that pulled the sleep pod into the ship. Silenna followed it up and helped Elora store the pod in a rear compartment.

The vessel accommodated ten passengers with two rows of five seats each and two seats in the cockpit for a pilot and co-pilot. The interior featured smooth yellow seats with a black mesh material lining the floor and low ceiling. Sitting in his seat, Logan noticed his anxiety level decreasing. The longer he sat there, the more relaxed he felt. He wondered if it had anything to do with the aliens or their ship. Whatever the case, he welcomed the relief.

Elora helped them strap into their seats. The belts fit loosely and the alien-sized seats gave them too much room to slide around. She handed them transparent plastic pillows to fill the empty spaces and showed them how to hold on to the seat and chest straps when the ship accelerated.

Elora and Silenna sat up front — going through a pre-flight check list, Logan imagined. With all its lurking dangers, he wanted his people out of the Siloe Patera crater sooner than yesterday. After about five minutes, Silenna powered up the engines. Elora activated the protective energy shield. It created a slight distortion to the view from the cockpit windows. The craft rose slowly and steadily to the surface. Logan spotted their rover in the parking area near the rim of the crater. A miner robot stood guard next to it. The robot opened fire at the ship, but the vessel moved away too quickly for the laser blasts to even reach the shields. Through the cockpit window, Logan watched the red Martian sands slip away underneath the nose of the skiff as it skimmed its way towards the sanctuary of the mother ship.

From sheer exhaustion and the relaxing vibe inside the cabin, he closed his eyes and quickly fell asleep.

*His mother lay in a coma with tubes streaming from her nose. Her face appeared as white as the sheets covering her emaciated body. Most of her long and lustrous black hair had fallen out. The gray splotches around her eye sockets made her look like an assault victim. At the bedside, seven-year-old Logan Carlson sobbed uncontrollably until his father slapped his arm. The tall, lean man brought his angular, crimson-tinged face to Logan's eye level. "Quit it," he said. "Cryin' won't make her better."*

*"I wish you were dying and not mom," Logan said.*

*His father grabbed him by both arms. "You little bastard. Don't ever say anything like that to me again."*

*Sitting in a wooden chair in the corner of the VA hospital room, his older sister, Stephanie, began crying.*

A stranger's voice called to him from far away. His eyes fluttered open. It startled him when he remembered they were in an alien ship.

*"We're home,"* Elora was saying.

He sat up in his seat, just in time to glimpse the enormous mother ship. It was a replica of the skiff, but much larger, from the tip of its nose, past the sweeping mid-wings, to the boomerang wing in the rear. Seconds later, the skiff hovered above the giant fuselage. From the cockpit window, Logan watched a section of the ship slide open. Silenna eased the skiff down into a hangar below.

*Yes,* Logan thought. *We're home. How strange to call an alien ship home?*

# MARS—ALIEN SHIP

AS LOGAN AND the others disembarked from the skiff, a stranger met them at the bottom of the stairs. He introduced himself as Dmitri Semerov and welcomed them aboard.

"Silenna told me about you." Logan introduced himself and his team. They all shook hands.

"I understand you single-handedly saved the surviving crew members. I admire your courage."

"I didn't save them single-handedly, Commander. Jon Henderson helped me, along with the ship's artificial intelligence program. Jon died in a battle with one of Kaminsky's robots."

"I'm sorry to hear that. When we have time, I'd like to hear your story."

"I look forward to it," Dmitri said.

The bright white interior of the hangar transmitted an energy field similar to the one he experienced in the skiff. The field buoyed Logan's energy and mood. It felt too good to be harmful. Then it hit him: *These aliens live in a higher energy field than we do. They've evolved into a higher consciousness. They tend to elevate the consciousness of other sentient beings they interact with. I don't know how I know that. I just know it. The knowing has something to do with the energy field.*

While he considered the mysterious source of this information, more intuitive understanding came to him.

*It's not the ship that emits the field. It's the aliens that transmit it. The field builds up in spaces the aliens regularly inhabit until it becomes noticeable. Wow!*

Logan heard Elora and Silenna stepping down from the skiff behind them. He turned in time to watch them maneuver the sleep pod onto the deck.

"Where did you find that?" Dmitri asked with an open-handed gesture toward the pod.

"In the storage rooms," Kate answered, "along with machinery from the crashed ships and a big stash of alien fuel ingots."

Dmitri looked confused.

Elora left them with the sleep pod in tow. Silenna joined their circle. She crossed her arms. The alien captain seemed content to stand with them without attempting to communicate.

"I think Silenna is standing guard to make sure we don't break anything," Rashawn said.

"Or waiting impatiently to give us the grand tour," Logan said.

Logan noticed Dmitri's serious expression. Apparently, he had no desire to share in their banter. "Why would the corporation store alien fuel in large quantities?"

"Because Micromium is not an ore indigenous to Mars," Kate explained. "It is alien fuel from the ships that crashed here. The mining operation is a sham. The corporation is covering up the truth to protect their investment."

"They only told us about the ships," Dmitri said. They didn't say anything about fuel. We all agreed to keep quiet about the ships because Benjamin Caliphas promised us a generous share of the profits that his new company stood to reap from the alien technology we recovered."

"What *really* happened to Jesse MacMahn and Anna Petrovsky?"

Logan asked. "We found their suits in the second storage room. They showed no damage. Kaminsky told me he recycled the suits."

Dmitri looked down and then up at Logan with a pained expression. "Caliphas ordered Jesse and Anna killed when they refused to go along with the scheme. Kaminsky floated the cover story about them dying in a random meteorite shower. Then he told all of us about the murders after he used the robot miners to do the dirty work. The murders locked us in tighter. We became accessories to murder after the fact. There was no way out."

"Why would Kaminsky keep their suits in the storage rooms?"

"He kept them there to remind us what would happen to us if we lost our nerve. He called it a truth and soul session. Anyone with second thoughts got an escort down to the rooms for a look at those suits. It worked."

Dmitri dropped his gaze to the hangar floor again, unable to meet the incredulous eyes of his audience.

Logan shook his head and put a hand on Dmitri's shoulder. "You saved three alien crew members. You broke away from the mining staff and now you're helping us. You can testify against the corporation when the time comes. You have a way out."

"I'll never forgive myself for what I did." Dmitri put a hand over his eyes and began sobbing. Silenna put a forefinger under his chin and made him look up. "*You are a good man,*" she reminded him.

Logan thought for a moment. With the addition of murder to the list of MMI's crimes, the danger to the audit team rose even higher. The corporation would do anything to stop them from making their report to the WEC. The time horizon had shrunk to zero. *Crisis management (in this case imminent death) usually simplifies matters. Funny how that works. We need to file our report and blast off.*

He turned to Silenna. *"Is there some way we can use your ship to transmit a report containing documents, videos, and photos?"*

*"There's no way to know if the documents and images would transfer coherently,"* she replied. *"And even if it worked, I'm sure the unusual electronic signature would raise questions."*

*Right. Dumb question,* Logan thought. "Dmitri, can we use the Communications Array to transmit our report?"

"Yes, but you need the code to get in."

"Our interstellar friends have a device that can crack the code."

He turned again to Silenna. *"After we get some rest, we need to break into the Communications Array at the mining colony and make our report to Earth. Will you take us there and bring us back to the ship when we're done?*

Silenna regarded him evenly with inquisitive eyes that blazed with energy from within her powerful body. After what seemed to Logan like an hour, she gave her reply.

*"You are a hard man to refuse. I will do as you ask, against my better judgment."*

Silenna showed them to their rooms in the crew quarters. Logan's room felt like a hotel suite compared to the cramped quarters of the mining base. Silenna demonstrated how to use the amenities. Wishing him a good night's rest, she left to help Rashawn and Kate get settled.

He needed a bath desperately. It had been days since his last shower. He practically ripped his suit and undergarments off to relax in a machine that wrapped around his body like a tobacco plant. The bath cleansed and disinfected his body with subtle waves of scintillating energy. He felt it soothing every muscle, sinew, and pore in his bone-tired body. Without realizing it, he fell into a dreamless sleep.

A pattern of high-pitched tones woke him. Logan had no idea how long he had been asleep. Remembering Silenna's tutorial, he identified the tones as a door bell. Someone wanted to see him. He forced himself to unfold from the luxurious alien bath. Draping himself in a silky yellow towel, he answered the door. Kate stood there, wearing a similar towel and a half-smile.

"What can I do for you?"

"Invite me in."

"We should be resting."

"We can rest together."

The emptiness and the darkness rose inside him like a ghostly specter. Sadness embraced him with cold arms. Where did these feelings come from?

They made love slowly and passionately on a bed big enough for three people. Afterwards, they held each other, hardly speaking a word. Her physical presence sparked something in him. He could no longer imprison his emotions. His mouth spoke words without his permission.

"It hurts to be close to you."

She placed her hand in the middle of his chest. "What do you mean?"

"There's a place inside me I don't want to go. If I go there, I'll drown, but that place opens every time I'm near you like this."

"What's in the place you can't go?"

"Darkness. Sadness. Pain. Anger."

"It's emotional trauma, Logan."

"Trauma?"

"Yes. 'Trauma' isn't too strong a word to describe it. It usually results from early childhood experiences. As we get older, we try to seal off those difficult experiences with various coping strategies. At our core, humans are highly sensitive instruments. We break easily, especially children who are too young to protect themselves."

"You seem to know to know a lot about it."

"I minored in Psychology as an undergrad. We had a whole course devoted to emotional trauma and its effect on individuals and society. Everyone carries some degree of trauma. Birth itself is a traumatic experience. Kids teased me mercilessly about my height all the way through high school. My mother never supported my dreams. She wanted me to choose a traditional female vocation. Without my father's encouragement, I wouldn't be lying in your bed."

He smiled.

"Logan, you can't repress those memories and the feelings associated with them. The tangle of emotions will eventually surface in self-destructive patterns if you don't deal with it."

"I can't live this way any longer."

"Admitting that is the first step towards healing. I'll help you find the right treatment."

He began shaking. She held his head to her breast and stroked his hair. "It's all right. I'll help you find the help you need when we get out of this."

He felt like a child. He felt the tears he never shed well up inside him, but he couldn't cry. Not now. He kissed her deeply and felt their connection. He made love to her with complete abandon. They made love more tenderly this time, until the final thrusts of their ecstatic, shared climax.

They lay together, exhausted. The ghosts and demons retreated to their dark lair, repelled by the burst of light he and Kate had just shared. It felt good. It felt right, but he knew the ghosts and demons were only hiding. He knew they would come back again with their teeth drawn. If only this could last...

They slept until the bed woke them.

After a good morning kiss, Logan said: "I want you to stay here while we make the report."

"No chance."

"Someone with detailed knowledge of the situation needs to stay out of the line of fire in case the rest of us don't make it. You're the logical candidate. We'll leave you here with a complete copy of the report."

"In case we don't make it. You say that like you're going out for groceries. If I die, no big deal; just carry on."

"Kate."

Brushing his lips, Kate slipped out of the bed, donned her towel, and left for her quarters. After the door closed behind her, the creatures from the pit began whispering to him. *Don't get close to her. She'll hurt you. Stop acting like a baby. Be a man.*

Ignoring the voices, Logan dressed slowly, methodically thinking through the steps needed to execute the raid on the Communications Array.

*   *   *

"Here's what I want you to do," Benjamin Caliphas said.

At the screen in the Communications Array, Oscar Kaminsky listened intently.

"There are only three places Marchant and his team will show up to make their report to the WEC. They'll either do it here, at the base, or aboard their ship."

"This whole thing is out of our control now, Benjamin. Committing more crimes won't help."

"You've made two mistakes, Oscar. You interrupted me and you've lost sight of the big picture. The technology we license will alleviate suffering and enhance the lives of billions of people on Earth and the lives of future generations on Mars. We must see this through. We've sacrificed. We deserve to be rewarded."

Oscar closed his eyes. If only he could make this all go away with the wave of a magic wand. He kept having the fantasy of being a kid again; only this time with the knowledge of what certain decisions would lead to.

"I can't do this anymore."

"Stop thinking of yourself. Think of the loyalty of your team. They've followed you this far. You can't quit on them now."

Oscar knew if he refused to cooperate with Caliphas, someone else would... and he'd disappear mysteriously somewhere in the line of duty.

"What do you want me to do?"

Kaminsky listened to Benjamin's plan.

"What about the aliens?"

"There are only two of them left. They have what they came for. Maybe they'll go back home. If not, I'll find a way to deal with them. The aliens aren't your problem. Focus on what, you have to do."

Oscar nodded. He had more work to do. Very dirty work.

# Chapter 28

# MARS—COMMUNICATIONS ARRAY

THE SKIFF BLASTED across the Martian plains towards the Communications Array. Silenna piloted the ship expertly. Logan rode alongside her in the co-pilot's chair. She flew manually, using a stick with a half-circle steering wheel that protruded from the control panel. Transparent orbs bearing unintelligible readings floated inside housings in the control panel. The ship spoke occasionally to Silenna in the Anelayan tongue. She occasionally slowed the craft to make tight turns or to rise above irregularities in the terrain. He hoped the ship's ground-hugging trajectory kept the skiff off the mining colony's sensitive detection system.

"*The ship senses a dust storm coming from the northeast,*" Silenna told him. "*We have two hours and fifty-six minutes to finish the mission and return to the ship.*"

"*We'll be in and out within a half hour,*" Logan said confidently.

The dome of the Communications Array hove into view as Silenna maneuvered the skiff around the wall of an extinct volcano. Inside the semicircle of the mountain wall, the Communications Array glittered in the Martian sun like a golden egg supported by four struts. A ladder reaching to the ground from the underside offered entry to workers equipped with the correct pass codes. With any luck, they would find the egg unstaffed. Formal communications meetings with Earth and scheduled maintenance happened infrequently. The Array served mainly as a backup station to the communications equipment at the mining base.

Silenna guided the skiff close to the underside of the egg. She set the ship down. It settled with the slightest bump.

Silenna wished them good luck. Soon, Logan, Rashawn, and Dmitri stood at the bottom of the ladder. Logan led the other two up. At the underside, Logan used the same device Elora had used to retrieve the pass code to the storage rooms. Logan made four unsuccessful attempts to retrieve the entry code. Mentally, he ran through Silenna's instructions about operating the device. On the fifth attempt, he had the code. Opening the outer airlock door, they moved into the atmospheric normalization chamber.

After a five-minute air pressurization cycle, they climbed the stairs leading up into the central array. With weapons drawn, they passed empty work cubicles on both sides. No sounds or voices filtered down from above. Logan motioned for Rashawn and Dmitri to remain behind. Quietly, he climbed the last few steps and peeked over the edge of the floor. No signs of life. Good.

Using his suit's intercom, he called to Dmitri and Rashawn. "We're clear. C'mon up."

Having reached the main floor without incident, they readied their materials and positioned themselves to transmit their report. After accessing the computer pass code, Logan loaded the files and began transmitting. Dmitri helped him monitor the transmission while Rashawn transmitted a duplicate report from another station. They anticipated a twenty-minute transmission and then a hasty retreat to the skiff.

Through the panoramic window beyond the transmitting stations, Logan saw the skiff rise to eye level. Silenna waved one arm back and forth inside the cockpit and then made a throat-cutting gesture. Logan interpreted her gesture as a warning to get out of the array.

Standing at the adjacent station, Dmitri had also witnessed Silenna's gesture.

"Keep transmitting," Logan said.

Rashawn looked up from his screen. "What's going on?"

Logan walked to the window. Three rovers ringed the ladder. "We have company."

"How many?" Dmitri asked.

"I can't see them. Maybe twelve, judging from the size of the rovers. They brought the big ones."

They heard the interior hatch open from downstairs. Boots stomping on metal echoed from the stairwell.

Logan motioned for Dmitri and Rashawn to move away from the transmitting stations. They crouched in defensive positions on opposite sides of the room behind matching bulkheads.

Logan watched the power to the transmitting machines die, one by one. Someone below knew how to cut the power from one of the work stations lining the stairs. So much for their comprehensive report to the WEC. Bastards. He wanted to scream. He wanted to blast every one of them into oblivion with Elora's shiny six-shooter.

"Stay here," he called to Dmitri and Rashawn. Logan crawled towards the stairwell. He stopped in the middle of the blue rubber floor.

He changed the channel on his intercom. "We can talk about this or fight. If anything happens to us, you'll have a lot of questions to answer. It's your choice."

"We want to talk."

Logan recognized the voice: William Rodgers, Chief Software Engineer and Kaminsky's second in command.

Rising from the floor, he hurried to the window to wave Silenna off. He didn't want her to attack the rovers or endanger her ship or her life. She understood and piloted the skiff away towards the hills and the mother ship.

A white flag crested the top of the stairwell, followed cautiously by the emerging figure of William Rodgers. Two other men appeared from the stairs and assumed positions on either side of him. Either the assault unit numbered less than Logan had anticipated, or rein-forcements waited in the stairwell.

"How many are you?" Logan asked.

"You don't want to find out," Williams answered. "Would you mind asking the rest of your team to come out from cover? We're standing here like sitting ducks."

"First, tell me why the three of you are here."

"For starters, it's our outpost. We belong here. You don't."

Logan waited.

"Kaminsky says he'll let you transmit your report from the base if the WEC agrees to grant the corporation and all of us full immu-nity."

"Why would they do that?"

"We'll kill every damn one of you including the lady doctor if they don't. We won't go down without a fight."

Logan thought it over. Kaminsky's men had them outnumbered, and the thought of Kaneko alone at the base made the decision clear. He called Rashawn and Dmitri out from their positions.

Kaminsky's men escorted them down the stairs. At the bottom stairwell, Logan felt a sharp jab in his right shoulder. He staggered and then fell into a bottomless, dark tunnel.

# Chapter 29

# MARS—AMERICAN HERITAGE

LOGAN AWOKE WITH the feeling that someone had stuffed his head with cotton balls.

He found himself strapped into the command seat of the American Heritage with a recorded countdown sounding in his ears. He listened to the simulated voices of Kate, Rashawn, and Kaneko greenlighting the checklist for each stage of the countdown. Kaneko and Rashawn lay strapped in their seats, fast asleep, on either side of him. No one wore space helmets.

The counterfeit launch sequence wore down inexorably while he struggled with the control console to abort it. The buttons did not respond. Someone had locked in the launch routine to auto-pilot. He tried to unlock the console with verbal commands using his credentials. No luck. He repeatedly punched the harness release mechanism in the center of his chest. It remained stubbornly on auto-lock.

Rashawn shifted in his seat. He groaned. Logan heard a rustling sound from the fourth seat behind them. His restraints prevented him from turning around to see who was back there.

"Is that you, Kate?"

No response. More rustling. *It's not Kate,* he remembered as the fog parted in his mind. *I told her to stay behind on the mother ship.*

Logan wasted no time. He opened a pocket in his utility belt. He found the alien decoder. Kaminsky's minions had apparently loaded them on the ship without taking the time to search them thoroughly. Why search a crew destined for execution? Kaminsky considered them already dead. Who needs a space helmet on a one-way ride to oblivion?

He knew there was no time to contemplate the details of their execution. It would appear to be some horrible accident. *We have to get out of here—fast.*

Logan used the decoder to recover the secret launch codes. He quickly aborted the launch by speaking the codes in sequence into the ship's computer. The auto-lock of his seat harness clicked to manual mode.

Removing the restraints, he rose to untie Rashawn's straps first. The sight of the robot emerging from the rear seat almost made him scream. It held two syringes menacingly in each hand. *He's here to keep us sedated until the accident happens.*

Rashawn staggered up from his seat. Despite a thudding headache, Logan felt reasonably in charge of his faculties. Although he looked groggy, Rashawn reacted to the danger smartly in the close quarters of the command cabin. Fishing a ten-inch wrench from his utility belt, he smashed the make-shift weapon into the robot miner's head. The attack temporarily staggered the robot, but the durable plastic composite protecting its brain cushioned the blow. The robot turned to face Rashawn. Logan had already drawn his wrench. He brought it down sharply on the skeletal column supporting the miner's head. The machine froze. Carefully skirting the needles, Rashawn joined Logan. They worked feverishly to revive Kaneko.

With Kaneko now on her feet, they found extra helmets in the living quarters below the command module. Before sliding downstairs, Logan thought he had glimpsed a subtle movement of the robot's arm. Looking up, he saw the robot's head appear in the opening to the command module.

Rashawn held Kaneko while Logan opened the exit airlock. Inside the pressure chamber, they heard the robot banging against the interior door. Bulging dents appeared on their side of the door.

The outer door opened as the inner door gave way. The robot poked its head through. Rashawn withdrew his wrench and smashed the thing in its neck again. The robot withdrew back into the ship.

While she gradually recovered consciousness, they helped Kaneko down the stairs to the Martian soil.

Logan scanned the terrain for cover. He expected the robot miner to make its way out of the airlock any second.

Three rovers appeared on the horizon.

"Something tells me it's not a rescue party," Rashawn said.

"Let's head for that ice and rock formation over there," Logan said, pointing.

They ran for the shelter of the icy formation thirty meters away.

Behind them, the American Heritage exploded into a fireball. They watched helplessly on the barren plain as, seconds later, pieces of the ship's wreckage crashed into the Martian soil, raising clouds of dust.

"They fucking blew up our ride," Rashawn said incredulously.

"The good news is we weren't in it. I'm sure the phony transmission Kaminsky cooked up was supposed to make it look like the ship exploded during lift off."

The rovers crested the northern horizon, growing larger and deadlier with each passing second.

*We're out of options,* Logan thought.

Kaneko, now fully conscious, pointed towards the western horizon. "Look."

Barely visible on the horizon, the skiff hurtled towards them, hugging the barren plain.

Oblivious of the oncoming alien ship, the rovers rushed at them from the north.

The skiff accelerated, eating up the distance between them and raising a dust trail.

"That alien hot rod is fast, but it looks like the rovers will reach us first," Rashawn said.

Logan put a reassuring hand on Rashawn's shoulder. There was nothing else he could do.

As if it had heard Rashawn, the skiff veered off in the direction of the rovers. It fired warning shots in front of the oncoming column. The blue energy bursts raised plumes of dust.

The rovers barreled through the dust screen.

"They must think whoever is piloting the ship is bluffing," Logan said.

"Have you seen any evidence of bad intentions from the aliens?" Rashawn said.

"Not yet, but there's always hope."

The rovers bore down on them. It reminded Logan of the old Mad Max movies from his boyhood. *Here come the savages.*

They watched from behind the icy rock formation. It promised only temporary refuge, unless the alien ship intervened.

The skiff emitted a thin blue rope of light from its rear mounted boomerang wing. The lead rover disintegrated into a ball of what looked like silver confetti that dissolved harmlessly into the thin Martian atmosphere.

Logan watched the ship fire another blue energy rope that disintegrated the second rover. The third rover came to a skidding halt. Turning, it headed in the opposite direction towards the mining base over the horizon.

The three of them emerged from behind the rock formation, waving and walking towards the skiff. Kaneko labored to keep up.

"Are you okay?" Logan asked her.

She held up a hand. "I'll be fine. I may have suffered a slight concussion. Nothing serious."

Banking nimbly, the skiff glided towards them and settled. A set of stairs descended from underneath the fuselage.

Kate came out to meet them.

"I thought you were supposed to stay on the ship," Logan said.

"When Silenna told me you were in trouble, I had to come with her."

"You disobeyed a direct order."

"I'm sorry, sir."

"At least your timing was good."

They boarded the skiff.

*"Strap in quickly,"* Silenna said. *"The dust storm is approaching and gathering strength. Every second is critical."*

The quiet, powerful engines and the onboard guidance system whisked the craft over the irregular Martian terrain in an arcing trajectory towards the mother ship. Silenna's remark echoed in Logan's mind: *"Every second is critical."*

# Chapter 30

# MARS—MOTHER SHIP

OSCAR KAMINSKY HAD never seen a Martian storm like the leviathan heading towards the mining base. He watched it gathering momentum in the distance through the panoramic window in the Operations Array. His weather app predicted it would hit the Communications Array in fifteen minutes. A system of three concentric energy shields encircled the Array and the mining base, protecting them from meteor showers, dust storms, and rough weather. The Communications Array had sustained damage from a few of the previous storms and meteorite showers passing through, but never anything serious. A few storms had torn through the outer shield before heading off harmlessly and blowing themselves out.

Something told him the time had arrived to send the video files he had been keeping for a rainy day back to the WEC and NASA.

Oscar sent the files with a carefully worded cover letter. Ten minutes later, he watched the storm smash into the Communications Array. At first, it withstood the onslaught. In the next moment, it disappeared in a shower of lightning bolts generated by the exploding energy shields. The storm had torn through the three-ply shields like toilet paper. It spat pieces of the outpost from the crown of a swirling funnel that looked to be gathering into a full-blown tornado.

For a chilling second, Oscar remembered the story of Captain Ahab watching a white whale breach the turbulent waters of the Pacific Ocean. Minutes later, the storm tore through the shields surrounding the mining base. A bolt of electricity exploded Oscar's panoramic window. When the bolt hit him with hellish force, Kaminsky screamed before the talon of electricity turned him into a smoldering skeleton.

\* \* \*

From the command deck of the mother ship, Logan watched the storm approaching. Dark clouds of swirling dust stretched across the horizon. The electronic screen in the cockpit displayed the storm and an estimated time of arrival in alien numerals. The thin Martian atmosphere was not supposed to sustain storms with the kind of destructive power this one promised. This thing was an anomaly. It was technically impossible. Yet, there it was, tearing up the terrain and charging at them like an army of furious Rhinos.

*"We have an eighteen-minute launch window,"* Silenna advised Logan and the others. *"Prepare for takeoff."*

Before he died, Logan learned, Galatar had devised a special harness system to secure human passengers in the over-sized seats on the command deck. Silenna had foreseen the need to transport Logan and his team in the event something happened to the American Heritage. Force of habit, Silenna explained to Logan, had prompted her to ask Galatar to create the backup system. Deep space exploration demanded redundant systems. One primary rule applied: always plan for the worst.

Unfortunately, no one had foreseen the sudden appearance of a killer storm that, according to all available scientific knowledge, had no right to exist.

Logan noticed Silenna looking up periodically to check on the violent storm through the windshield.

*"Will your shields hold up?"*

*"I doubt it."*

He sat there feeling helpless as Silenna prepared the ship for flight. He expected to see Elora sitting in the co-pilot's chair. *She must be doing something important below deck*, he concluded.

The boiling storm devoured the natural light of the Martian plain until it cloaked the ship in total darkness.

"*Five minutes to liftoff*," Silenna announced.

That left them roughly ten minutes of leeway, Logan calculated. In the seat next to him, Kate clutched his hand. Dmitri and Rashawn evidently sensed the intimate nature of their relationship. They no longer tried to cover it up. Desperate circumstances reduced the need for artifice in human relationships. Death stalked them, circling ever closer. Their instincts sharpened. They directed every ounce of energy to a single goal: survival at all costs.

Silenna called the launch down to zero.

The ship lurched upwards. Silenna maneuvered the thrusters to trim their ascent. She spoke in her native tongue into a communication device inside her lightweight translucent helmet. Silenna nodded in response to a masculine voice from below. Logan figured the voice belonged to the alien captain they had rescued from a slow death in the storage rooms. Thank the stars Elora and Silenna had exercised the compassion and foresight to save him. They needed him now.

"*Is there a problem?*" Kate asked.

"*The response is a bit sluggish*," Silenna replied. "*It's within an acceptable range. When we reach orbit, we'll attend to it.*"

Silenna guided the ship away from the storm while lifting the nose gradually. The ship hovered somewhere above the Martian surface, awaiting the command to ignite its powerful engines. Logan wondered if a gauntlet of G forces awaited them, or if the advanced propulsion system would spare them the ordeal.

Silenna said something into her helmet. Logan's heart sank as the ship began to lose its launch angle.

"*Our engines are non-responsive*," Silenna announced calmly. "*The storm is affecting the ignition system.*"

"*How much time do we have?*" Dmitri asked.

*"I can keep moving away from it, but eventually it will grab us if we can't restore ignition."*

Through the walls of the ship, Logan heard the winds screaming with the intensity of what sounded like a category five hurricane. The storm had formed into an immense tornado, tearing long swatches of rock and sand from the surface and spinning it up into the atmosphere.

They had to launch soon, before the storm consumed them.

Silenna spoke directly into the comm link of her helmet, coordinating her efforts with her crew mates in the bowels of the ship. Logan assumed Elora and the captain were working feverishly to bring the ship's powerful engines back to life.

He watched Silenna struggle to keep the ship out of the clutches of the approaching maelstrom.

The ship shuddered violently against the outer bands of the storm. They were toast if the churning dust column came any closer. He turned to Kate. She had closed her eyes—not a bad idea.

Silenna angled the ship back into launch position. The ship turned on its axis. The wind howled like a chorus of werewolves. Kate's grip on his hand tightened.

The engines fired, pressing Logan deep into his seat. The G forces built until he thought his heart would explode.

The ship cleared the grasping arms of the storm. Gulping down mouthfuls of oxygen, Logan felt the G forces abate. He looked over to Kate. Her eyes fluttered open. Struggling to breathe, she coughed spasmodically.

Logan helped her to breathe by massaging her chest. Gradually, her breathing and vital signs returned to normal.

"I blacked out," she said.

"Are you okay?"

"I think so."

Logan turned to Dmitri and Rashawn across the aisle. They gave him a thumbs-up despite looking like a couple of disheveled stunt men who had kayaked over Niagara Falls and lived to tell about it.

"*Sorry for the rough ride,*" Silenna said. "*Our launch protocol is usually a lot more comfortable.*"

"No problem," Rashawn said. "*I'd rather be alive than dead and comfortable.*"

When they reached orbit, Silenna put the ship on auto pilot. "*I'll show you to the crew quarters. You can eat, rest, and bathe while I adjust the thrusters and make a final evaluation of the ship's systems.*"

Six hours later, they sat behind Silenna, awaiting the launch from Mars orbit.

"*The voyage to Earth will take approximately twenty minutes in your time,*" Silenna explained. "*With any luck, the ride will be less eventful than the Mars liftoff.*"

"*You promise?*" Rashawn deadpanned.

"*We'll drop you off in a remote area close to a small town to avoid detection,*" Silenna told them.

"Understood," Logan replied. "*I have a satellite phone to call in a rescue team. We'll be fine. What are your plans after you leave us?*"

"*We're going back to Aneleya. We've learned how to prevent the fuel contamination problem from occurring again.*"

"*What about terraforming Mars?*"

"*After taking inventory, we found that the caretaker unit blew up vital replacement parts for the terraforming machines. Completing the second objective of our mission isn't possible.*"

After absorbing Silenna's disappointing news, Logan said: "*I'd like your permission to video record the three of you and the ship to include in our report. Our superiors will expect some visual proof that you exist.*"

"*I can't honor your request,*" Silenna said. *The fact that you made it home without your ship will have to be enough proof. You can keep the decoding device as a token of our friendship. That by itself will back up your story.*"

"*Why can't we record you?*" Kate pressed.

"*Now that that we've decided not to terraform Mars, my standing orders are to depart without leaving behind any evidence of our presence. I've already disobeyed those orders. By giving you the decoding device, I'm leaving you with a handshake and a wink.*"

Logan turned to Kate and Rashawn. They looked back at him with knowing smiles and a shrug of the shoulders. They knew what lay ahead: endless questions by NASA scientists, lie detector tests; maybe an investigation by a top-secret Senate commission and WEC members. Oh, what fun!

He experienced the ride home as literally a blur. The ship shot through a hole its Micromium-powered engines tore in the space-time continuum. Silenna parked the ship in a high Earth orbit. They used the skiff to complete the journey in a less conspicuous manner.

Under the cover of nightfall, the shuttle craft settled in a potato field less than a mile away from a farm house. Logan anticipated a few UFO reports. There might be a few video recordings. No matter what precautions they undertook, no one could prevent the possibility of sightings.

In the moonlit night, the sight of a dozen military vehicles rumbling into the potato field and heading directly towards the skiff quickly shattered his expectations.

Heavily armored vehicles equipped with high energy laser weapons surrounded the skiff.

"How did they find us so quickly?" Kate wondered aloud.

"Don't know, but I'm sure we'll find out," Logan said.

Silenna turned to him. "*You said the people of Earth are not like the people from the corporation. What I see is more of the same.*"

"You stay in the ship," Logan answered. "*I think we can straighten this out.*"

After Silenna lowered the stairs, Logan and the others removed their helmets and met the ground forces with their hands raised in the air. A group of armed commandos rushed out to meet them. From behind, a heavily decorated officer approached.

Logan spoke up for the group. "Glad to meet you, sir. I'm Logan Marchant and this is my team. We've just arrived from Mars, and we have quite a story to tell." He introduced each team member with a brief description of their background and mission objectives.

The officer introduced himself as Captain Allan Morehead, a paunchy man in his forties with prematurely gray hair under his cap. "Your ship blew up, Commander. You're supposed to be dead."

"Sorry to disappoint you sir."

"You and these people, could be aliens in disguise for all I know."

"You'll have to take my word that I'm me or take X-rays, if you have a machine handy?"

"Scrap the attitude, Marchant. I'm placing you under arrest."

"For what?"

"We'll start with sexual misconduct and go from there."

Logan stood there stunned. *How could anyone know what happened between me and Kate behind closed doors?*

"In addition to your inappropriate behavior with a person under your command, Oscar Kaminsky reported an alien attack. The reported incident includes video footage of an alien vessel destroying rovers manned with MMI personnel. Our satellites and deep space radar stations have been on high alert ever since." He pointed to the mother ship. "We tracked that thing from the time it reached Earth orbit."

*Kaminsky reported Kate and me? How did he know about us?*

"The miners attacked us, Captain. They are criminally liable for murder and a conspiracy to defraud the WEC regarding the origins of the Micromium ore they've been shipping to Earth. We have a detailed report to file concerning the mining colony's activities. We'd like your assistance in transporting us to WEC Headquarters as quickly as possible."

"My orders are to investigate a UFO landing and take into custody anyone or anything that comes out of it."

Something behind him captured Morehead's attention. Logan turned to see Silenna descending the stairs of the skiff.

*"Commander Marchant is not an alien, Captain. I am. My name is Silenna. I am speaking to you telepathically with the help of a portable translation device. You need not be alarmed. Think what you want to say to me and I'll hear you."*

Silenna made her way gracefully to the Captain. She wore body clenching coveralls without any head gear. With only a few feet separating them, the alien's size and fitness lit up the sagging features of Morehead's pasty face.

The commandos raised their weapons.

Morehead held up a hand to the troops. "Stand down," he commanded.

*"I will come with you to offer my testimony to any court that holds these people in judgment."*

*"If you come with us, I can't promise anything. I'll turn you over to the authorities along with Commander Marchant and his team."*

Logan turned to Silenna. *"You don't want to do this. Go back to your ship."*

Ignoring him, Silenna turned to Morehead. *"I will go with you to your authorities."*

Chapter 31

# EARTH—AIR FORCE BASE

SILENNA SAT UNCOMFORTABLY on two wooden chairs in the cramped cinderblock room somewhere deep underground. She had allowed her captors to escort her to a military installation the Earthlings called Edwards Air Force Base. She had already lost her patience with the Martian Miners. The military representatives surrounding her had succeeded in wearing her patience even thinner. On her way to this miserable little room, her handlers had shown a pitiable lack of consideration and respect for a fellow intelligent life form. They had confiscated her space suit and replaced it with a hastily sewn together shirt and a pair of trousers made of course, drab-green material that irritated her skin. Fortunately, she still wore her space boots, thanks to a short supply of size twenty shoes made for six-toed people.

After a few fitful hours of sleep on three bare mattresses thrown together side-by-side, her captors had hustled her into this uninviting "debriefing room." From their curt attitudes, she assumed they considered her hostile and dangerous. She was beginning to think Commander Marchant and his team were the only civilized representatives of their race.

Having given the uninitiated audience a short tutorial on how the telepathic translation device worked, the interrogation began. She listened politely to a young intelligence officer who introduced himself as Johnathan MacDonald. Two scientists, a five-star general, and the head of an agency the Earthlings called the NSA waited to pose their questions after MacDonald.

MacDonald straightened two pieces of paper lying on the desk in front of him. Clearing his throat, he asked the first question on his carefully scripted list.

*"For the record, state your name and the purpose of your presence on Mars. Before you answer, it is my duty to inform you that this meeting and everything you say will be recorded."*

*"Thank you for your question, John MacDonald. You may call me Silenna. My real name is unpronounceable in your language.*

*"For your record, I wish to inform you that I am here to make a statement pertaining to Commander Marchant and his crew. I am not here to answer your endless questions."*

She waited a moment for the shockwaves of her telepathic bomb to subside. The men and women at the table looked at each other and then at her. No one, including MacDonald, seemed to know how to proceed.

Silenna knew exactly what to say and do.

*"Commander Marchant has a complete report concerning the activities of the mining colonists. When you review the report and its supporting exhibits, you will find that the colonists and their corporation, Martian Mining Interplanetary, are guilty of an immense fraud perpetrated on the member nations of the World Energy Council and the people of Earth.*

*"I take full responsibility, along with my crew, for the deaths of the six miners in Oscar Kaminsky's report. The miners attacked us in rovers to murder the audit team to prevent them from transmitting their report. This attack occurred after the miners blew up the audit team's spacecraft in a failed plot to execute them and then cover up their deaths. I watched the ship explode before its engines fired for*

*takeoff. Fortunately, the team escaped and we rescued them before the rovers could cut them down on the Martian plains. Commander Marchant and his team deserve a medal for their bravery and courage. They have done a great service to the people of Earth.*

*"My ship's computers translated the audit team's report. I've read it and state for the record that every word of it is true. The audit team and Dmitri Semerov will answer many of the questions you have about me, my people, and our mission on Mars. Because Dmitri Semerov spent more time than anyone else aboard our ship, you will find that he knows the most about us. Dmitri saved my life. Because of his unselfish actions, my crew and I saved your audit team.*

*"Now, with or without your permission, I will take my leave. I caution you against trying to stop me. The ship waiting for me in orbit can level this entire planet. I sincerely hope you do not choose to test this claim."*

She turned from MacDonald to Logan. *"Before leaving, I request a private meeting with Commander Marchant. Thank you for your time and attention. Goodbye."*

Silenna rose from the table. No one made a move to stop her from exiting the room. Without seeking permission from anyone, Logan followed her.

* * *

The elevator glided noiselessly on its way to the surface from the topsecret bunker. Feeling a tug of sadness, Logan readied himself for whatever Silenna wanted to tell him. He had made an extraordinary friend. The thought of losing the bond they shared weighed heavily on him.

*"I feel you deserve to know what I'm about to tell you. I don't want to leave you with any doubts or questions. I want you to know the whole story. What you do with it is up to you."*

Logan waited while the elevator rushed upwards.

*"Before we set off on our failed mission to file your audit report*

*from the Communications Array, I gave Elora instructions to recover the fuel and the other remains of our doomed ships from the storage rooms in the crater. Elora landed the mother ship outside the entrance to the mine. With the ship's gravity gun, we intended to float the cargo out of the caves and into an onboard storage bay. Elora entered the mine to plant a single device in each room to network the recovery process."*

Silenna paused for a moment. For the first time, Logan saw emotion well up in her eyes.

*"Elora warned Kaminsky not to interfere. When no robots showed up at the caves, Elora assumed Kaminsky and whomever he reports to had taken her seriously. When she entered the first storage room, someone set off a series of explosive charges. Elora was buried, along with everything else in the rooms. The captain we rescued from the first mission had stayed in the ship to work the gravity gun. He flew the ship out of the crater when Elora's vital signs flat-lined.*

*"Kaminsky and the mining corporation took revenge on us for meddling in their affairs and literally buried all of the damning evidence at the same time. Your people have a phrase for it: killing two birds with one stone."*

Something told him there was nothing he could say to console Silenna. He had a hard enough job himself absorbing the terrible news of Elora's untimely death.

The doors of the elevator opened into a long corridor. Two Marines waited outside for them. Logan stared at them. They stared back. In excellent physical condition, both Military Policemen stood stiffly at attention with their hands resting on energy pistols holstered at their sides. The MP to his left addressed him.

"Sir, our orders are to escort the alien back to her shuttle craft. You will wait here with us until the brass decides what to do with you."

Grappling with the tragedy of Elora's death, Logan paid no attention to the MP. He stumbled into the corridor in a whirlwind of emotions. Shock gave way to numbness, then deep sadness, and finally, hot anger. He felt ashamed to be a member of the same race as Kaminsky and his cohorts.

Gripping his weapon, the MP said, "Sir, I must ask you to step back into the elevator."

Silenna stepped from the elevator. Her size clearly made an impact on the two men standing in their way.

*"Tell them I wish to speak with you before I go with them."*

Logan forced himself to regain control of his thoughts and emotions. "She's not going anywhere until we finish our conversation. We speak telepathically. You can stay right here with us."

The Marines exchanged a look. Shrugging, the one on the left said, "Okay, finish your talk. You have five minutes."

In the distance, Logan saw a Marine in full parade dress enter the corridor.

He stepped away from the elevator with Silenna in tandem. Drawing their weapons and moving a respectful distance away, the MPs watched them intently. Then he heard her thoughts again.

*"When Kaminsky came aboard our ship, the AI determined that he had not downloaded the drawings and notes he was compiling of the technology he found in our crashed ships. His superiors wanted him to deliver the files personally rather than risk the chance of the transmission being intercepted."*

*"So, nobody gets the technology?"*

*"Yes. I made sure of it."*

*"What do you mean?"*

*"I started the dust storm with a weather simulator we use for terraforming. I aimed it directly at the mining colony. I fully intended to destroy the mining colony and its inhabitants. I am as guilty as Kaminsky and his bosses for wanting revenge. I acted from both rage and reason. I avenged the deaths of Elora and Galatar while obliterating all traces of our stolen technology. It is too dangerous to leave that kind of power in the hands of a race too unstable to wield it. As for my rage, it almost cost us our lives. I regret putting you and your team*

*in danger. I planned to harmlessly disperse the storm with the weather simulator. I did not expect it to grow out of control, fueled by the energy it absorbed from the colony's triple-strength perimeter shields."*

*"I don't know what to say, Silenna, except that I understand."*

*"You can't possibly understand the extreme sacrifices we made to come to your solar system. You may be wondering why we even bothered. The answer is simple. In the vastness of the universe, we have discovered only a few worlds suitable for sustaining our race. We have already colonized two worlds closer to our home planet. After all we've been through, I'm convinced something drew us to distant Mars besides its rich mineral resources and proximity to your sun, which make it an ideal terraforming candidate. I have a strong feeling the destiny of our races is somehow intertwined. I can't explain it, except to say we have much to offer your people and you must have something to offer us, although I can't imagine what that something might be."*

From her serious expression, Logan took it that Silenna intended no humor with her final comment. Unable to contain himself, he chuckled. There was nothing left to do but see the humor in the situation, or go crazy. The MPs looked askance at him.

Silenna kept staring at him with that serious expression.

*"Forgive me, Silenna. I mean no disrespect."*

Her eyes became curious.

*"You've seen some of the worst examples of human nature. I hope one day you'll have the chance to witness the remarkable goodness in our nature that allows us to endure and prosper."*

Her eyes softened. She seemed to want to say something, but she remained silent.

The Marine Logan had spotted earlier reached them. Coming to attention, he offered a crisp salute and introduced himself.

"Hello, Commander. I'm Corporal Jonas Glixt with the second airborne division. It's a pleasure to meet you, sir."

The two Military Policemen came to attention. Glixt put them at ease. He lost some of his composure after a long look at Silenna.

"What can I do for you, Corporal?"

"Sir, President Wilbourne has invited you and your team to the White House. He wants to hear your report in person. The lady alien is also invited."

Logan telepathically relayed the invitation to Silenna. Silenna took a moment to transmit her silent reply.

"The lady alien's name is Silenna. She appreciates the President's invitation, but she respectfully must decline it. Duty calls her back to her ship."

"Okay. How soon can you and your team be ready to leave for Washington?"

"Are you assuming my team wants to see the President, Corporal Glixt?"

"I suppose I assumed that, sir."

"Let me ask them and I'll get back to you."

"Very well, sir. I'll wait right here for the answer."

Logan stood facing Silenna awkwardly, unsure what to do. She stepped forward and engulfed him in a gentle, comradely embrace. *"I hope the stars bring us together again, my friend. Say goodbye to your team for me and give them my thanks."*

He found that he could not speak. Pulling away, she looked once more at him, smiled, and stepped away with the two MPs. He watched them disappear down the corridor.

"Are you all right, sir?"

"Give me a minute, Corporal, then I'll go down and see what the team wants to do."

# Chapter 32

# EARTH—SOMEWHERE IN EUROPE

IN A SECRET meeting at an undisclosed site, the multi-national dignitaries of the WEC convened at mid-day to hear the audit team present their report.

Dmitri, Rashawn, Kaneko, and Kate had already testified, accompanied by the video and photographic evidence captured during the mission. Their testimony proved to be convincing and damning, pointing a finger of guilt at Martian Mining Interplanetary for the high crimes of fraud, conspiracy, murder, and a litany of related charges. Logan stepped up to the podium to read the conclusions of the report. After a few minutes of introductory remarks, he moved into the heart of his presentation.

"The evidence clearly indicates that a future of clean energy is *NOT* upon us. The search must go on for economically feasible and environmentally safe energy sources. As you've seen, the risks of using Micromium far outweigh the benefits. Aside from the deleterious effects to machinery and the likelihood of fusion reactor accidents, our supply of Micromium is limited to what we already have in storage here. There will be no more shipments from Mars. Micromium, at best, is only a stop-gap solution to our problems.

"We must act quickly to completely phase out the use of fossil fuels. We have reached a threshold with two paths before us. One leads to the destruction of life on Earth as we know it. The other path leads us out of the hole we have dug for ourselves and into a future that restores the health of our biosphere and ensures our survival as a species.

"If we continue to pollute the environment, the damage we do will be irreparable. We can no longer kick the can down the road. It is our duty to communicate this message to the world and to guide every nation on Earth in the steps towards our environmental salvation."

After the applause died down, Jeremy Kornbluth of the WEC addressed the audit team.

"Please rise to hear the Council's decision regarding disciplinary actions stemming from the late Oscar Kaminsky's report supported by video evidence.

Logan's stomach tightened. He had not slept well during the ten days after the meeting with President Wilbourne. To Logan's surprise, the President had not mentioned anything about disciplinary actions. Wilbourne had simply thanked them for their service and presented them with a new medal created for exemplary achievement in outer space missions. Evidently, the President had chosen the role of "the good cop." Facing the WEC panel, Logan readied himself for the other end of the stick.

As he stood with the others, he felt a surprising sense of relief to be hearing, rather than anxiously awaiting, whatever judgment the council handed down. He could only hope that his affair with Kate would not cost them their careers. He glanced at Kate and their eyes met for one sweet moment.

Jeremey Kornbluth cleared his throat before speaking. "I'll begin with the question of the events surrounding the deaths of the six miners in the battle with the alien spacecraft. From your report and the testimony of the alien named Silenna, the evidence strongly suggests the miners attacked you with murderous intent to prevent you from filing your report. Since the entire mining staff perished in the dust storm, there is no one left to testify against you. Therefore, in regard to this matter, no charges will be filed against any of you by the WEC and NASA. This ruling also protects you from charges brought by any other criminal or civil court."

Logan quickly took an inventory of the expressions on the faces of his team and Dmitri. Everyone appeared deeply relieved. Although no one expected the charges to be handed over to a military court, it felt good to have them officially dismissed.

"Moving on to the matter of conspiracy to commit murder, this Council, in its capacity as sole arbitrator, has decided to drop the charge against Dmitri Semerov for his complicity in the deaths of Jesse McMahan and Anna Petrovsky. Since Mr. Semerov did not commit the murder and faced certain death if he reported it, we see no reason to punish him."

Upon hearing his muted sobs, Logan turned to Dmitri. Tears streamed down his cheeks. He sighed heavily before regaining his composure.

Logan silently congratulated the Council for their decision.

"As to the charge against Mr. Semerov for his role in the Micromium fraud, the Council has decided to sentence him to one thousand hours of community service. The criminal charges are dropped in consideration of his heroic efforts to save the alien crew, their ship, and consequently the lives of the audit team. He performed these duties in direct violation of the mining corporation's criminal orders and at great risk to his own life."

In response to Kornbluth's pronouncement, Dmitri collapsed backward into his chair. Kornbluth again cleared his throat.

"You haven't been dismissed, Mr. Semerov."

Wobbling out of his chair, Dmitri pulled himself to attention.

Kornbluth's gaze now focused on Logan and Kate.

"Now we come to the matter of sexual misconduct. For the record, the WEC and NASA made no attempt to invade the personal lives of the audit team. We assume Oscar Kaminsky, on his own or under orders, planted cameras in all the audit team members' rooms to keep tabs on what you were doing. For all we know, he did the same to everyone on the base. This is how we came into possession of what I can only term as very graphic evidence of improper conduct between an officer and a subordinate. Before I render the Council's decision, I'd like to hear something from both Commander Marchant and Corporal Blackstone explaining your behavior. You first, Commander."

"I really have nothing to say, Mr. Vice President, except that I was aware of my responsibilities and acted against my better judgment. I can only hope my actions will not negatively impact Corporal Blackstone's career."

Kornbluth nodded and turned to Kate.

"I'd like to take complete responsibility for the incident. I goaded Commander Marchant into having sex with me. I know it was wrong. There is no excuse for my behavior."

Jeremy Kornbluth clasped his hands and rested his head on them. He had a lion's mane of thick red hair and keen brown eyes staring out under bushy eyebrows.

"I agree with both of you. Your behavior is inexcusable. That said, you will not be disciplined for the incident. We intend to bury it. Why? Because we need heroes in the face of the terrible disappointment the world will experience when we announce that Micromium is not the source of clean energy that we hoped it would be.

"There will be a shit storm when the whole story comes out. The press and the politicians will be screaming for answers. Why wasn't the fraud discovered sooner? No one will care that Martian Mining Interplanetary did a masterful job of covering up the origins of the ore and its disabling effects on machinery. Our member nations counted on us to protect their interests. We failed them. We will have to answer for our failure. Our one saving grace is you. You aren't perfect, but you definitely *are* heroes for the job you did. The Council is grateful for your service. We will all live to fight another day.

"With that said, this meeting and these matters are officially closed. Good day to all."

# EPILOGUE

BENJAMIN HEARD THE thudding of heavy boots running in the marble hallway. He sat, motionless, at the desk of his penthouse office, staring straight ahead. He hadn't slept in the past thirty-six hours. He had been up for days before; running on adrenaline, excited about building his new company, radiating hope and enthusiasm to all who came in contact with him. Sleep loss never bothered him. The weariness he felt now sprang from his broken dreams and narrowing options. The malaise crept deeper and deeper into his troubled soul.

Using the inlaid computer at his desk, he had spent the last two hours remotely wiping all the files from his private server. There was only one thing left to do before the boots arrived at the outer door. There would be no staff to greet the FBI and SWAT teams. He had given them an extra day off the night before and wished them an enjoyable weekend. He had only one chore left to do.

He stood, feeling the stiffness in his legs from sitting so long, and unlocked the door to his terrace. A magnificent view of the Houston skyline greeted him. He had watched the sun rise from this very spot on so many glorious mornings.

The sound of the government team breaking down the expensive teak wood doors to his outer office startled him. He would miss the high seat of power that was his sanctuary—the place where he always knew his destiny would lead him. He would miss it all. *Alas, nothing lasts forever,* he told himself.

Benjamin swung his legs over the railing and stepped into oblivion.

✳ ✳ ✳

After a week-long debriefing, the audit team went their separate ways to recuperate. Logan and Kate stole away to a small horse farm owned by Kate's mother in Ocala, Florida. After rising early, they watched the morning edition of CNN while enjoying their breakfast of whole wheat pancakes, turkey sausage, and coffee.

"Good morning and welcome to the Kantor Report. I'm Adam Kantor, starting your day off with in-depth coverage of today's most pressing issues reported by our award-winning news team.

"In this morning's lead story, CNN has learned that Benjamin Caliphas, CEO of Martian Mining Interplanetary, committed suicide shortly after dawn by leaping from the terrace of his penthouse office suite, apparently in response to charges of corporate malfeasance, conspiracy to defraud government agencies, murder, and multiple related charges. Key employees of the corporation have been taken into custody for questioning, among them, Carl Haynes, Executive Vice President of Courtland Aerospace.

"Caliphas' death comes only three days after the WEC released the shocking news that the corporation's mining colony was decimated by a ferocious Martian dust storm. Satellite photos confirmed that none of the colonists survived. The SEC halted trading of MMI stock after shares plummeted on the news."

Logan turned off the program. It was old news to them. For the sake of their sanity, they had come to Bernice Blackstone's quiet farm for some badly needed R&R.

She took his hand and led him out to the porch where they watched young horses gamboling in the pasture with their dams looking on.

Rather than calm him down, the peace and quiet of the farm had stimulated a barrage of Logan's recent memories. He needed to talk to her about one of them.

"When I boarded the Anelayan ship, I had this intuition. I knew, somehow, that the Anelayans elevate the people they meet from other worlds. It's like they radiate something—a transformative energy. Do you think we've become better people from our contact with Silenna and the others?"

Kate turned and clasped her hands lightly on the back of his neck. Looking deeply into his eyes, she said, "I can't answer that, but I know one good thing that came out of our time on Mars."

"What would that be?"

"Us."

"I think you may have a point," he said.

They kissed.

He felt the darkness rising from the pit inside him. Could he ever give her what she deserved? He wanted to be the man she needed. She had convinced him that he had work to do to be that man.

He thought of Silenna, Elora and Galatar. Remembering their bravery and daring gave him the courage to try. He had an inkling they had inspired in him something else: a passionate desire to overcome the lurking monsters born from the childhood loss of his mother and an abusive relationship with his father. Hell, if he could fly into outer space, mix it up with the bad guys from MMI, deal with super-intelligent aliens, and come home in one piece to tell the story, he ought to be able to do anything—maybe even conquer his demons. Now he had a powerful reason.

He held her tightly.

She pulled back. "What are you thinking?"

"I'm glad we met."

"Is that all?"

"I know that you are big trouble."

They laughed.

He held her tighter. He never wanted to let her go.

# About the Author

After a career in marketing and business communications, David Gittlin began writing short stories, screenplays, and novels. His first two novels, *Three Days to Darkness and Scarlet Ambrosia,* are available online at Amazon and Barnes & Noble.

*Visit*
**www.davidgittlin.com** and **www.threedaystodarkness.com**
for book trailers and more information.

*Read the first chapter of*
***Scarlet Ambrosia*** *on the following pages.*

**SCARLET Ambrosia**

Blood is the Nectar of Life

**David Gittlin**

How does a nice, Jewish accountant tell his parents he's become a vampire? If only that were his biggest problem.

A one-night stand, an error in judgment, a wrong turn-words can barely describe the events that thrust Devon Furst into the arms of a beautiful vampire lover.

The violent aftermath of that fateful night threatens to burn Devon's eternal life down to ashes and endangers the lives of everyone close to him.

Everything in Devon's life changes in the span of a few hours. When he asks Mathilde de Roche one too many questions, the troubled vampiress has no choice but to offer Devon two terrible alternatives: Death or life as a vampire. For a man aged twenty-eight and in perfect health, death is not an option. Mathilde's alluring beauty makes the decision and her vampire blood easier to swallow.

Devon must leave behind everyone and everything he holds dear, to face a future full of uncertainty, and a five-hundred-year-old enemy endowed with super-human powers.

\* \* \*

"With so many vampire novels on the market today, one could wonder at the need for yet another; but *Scarlet Ambrosia* is a vampire story of a different color, seasoned not so much by the drama of blood-letting as by the more universal themes of self-discovery, human nature, and redemption. Ultimately this is what makes or breaks any genre; especially one such as the urban fantasy or vampire story, which too often tends to eschew self-examination in favor of high drama. And this is just one of the reasons why *Scarlet Ambrosia* stands out from the urban fantasy genre crowd."

—DIANE DONOVAN,
*Senior eBook Reviewer, Midwest Book Review*

# CHAPTER 1

OWNTOWN MIAMI BLAZED with life, even at ten o'clock in the
evening. The Miami Arena emptied thousands of Heat bas-
ketball fans into the streets after a mid-week night game.
Devon Furst wove through the oncoming crowd on his short walk to
Contour, a high-end fitness club where he worked out and met women.
The bright, colored lights of Bay Front Mall lent a carnival atmosphere
to the main drag of Biscayne Boulevard.

Earl Klugh's "Late Night Guitar" played through Devon's earbuds.
He found the smooth jazz helped to calm him down after a marathon
day of tax season deadlines. A faded Adidas gym bag bounced against
his hip. He hummed along with the music, passing "Coco-Loco-
Nuts," a trendy bar and grill Devon always avoided on his way to the
gym. Bars in general had lost their attraction for Devon. He had
given up drinking alcohol during his cocaine rehabilitation days.
Drinking had never been a problem for Devon, but after rehab, he
avoided any substance that might gain power over him. Alcohol ab-
stinence became the voluntary half of a package deal.

His father was the chairman of a powerful corporate law firm in
Miami. Devon made the grades and LSAT scores to get into Columbia
Law School. Three semesters later, he flunked out. A year of therapy

taught him that the best way to be successful and avoid self-destructive behavior was to stay out of his father's shadow. He had no desire to become a doctor or lawyer, so he chose accounting, the third most popular profession of adult Jewish males.

In therapy, Devon sought to understand and reconcile his competing drives. He wanted security and simultaneously craved adventure. He told himself he wanted to settle down while going through woman like the number two pencils he used at work. He felt a constant restlessness inside—a need for something more than what was in front of him. He had yet to find the elusive "something more." Perhaps the uneasy feeling had led to his addiction.

He hitched the Adidas bag up on his shoulder. The Contour building hove into view. He anticipated a decent crowd at the gym with enough good-looking women to keep him motivated to do his lower body workout. He hated leg exercises, and he was tired from the long day.

*When are you going to take some time to relax? Tax season will whittle you down to a splinter if you don't take some time to slow down.*

These thoughts crept into his mind, uninvited and without warning. He suddenly felt thirsty, as if he had just polished off a large tub of salted popcorn. He desperately needed a drink of water. He had drained the last of his water bottles at the office. No stores or small restaurants remained open at this hour. Coco-Loco-Nuts loomed as the only watering hole in sight.

Once inside, he ordered a large bottle of Perrier at the bar. The conversations of a roomful of people and a driving Latin beat reverberated like buzzing insects off the rosewood walls and factory-style, black-painted ceiling. The slinky bartender with straight black hair, Asian features, and too much eye makeup appeared with the sparkling water and a glass. Devon held up a hand.

"I'll just take the bottle with me," he said, placing a bill on the bar. "Keep the change."

"Let me get you a bag," the bartender said. "We're not supposed to let customers walk out with bottles. But hey, it's not alcohol, you tip big, and you're cute as hell." She winked at him and walked away. She had a very nice ass and long legs underneath her short black skirt. Devon felt a rise in his pants. It had been too long a day to start feeling horny. He couldn't wait to take a deep swig of Perrier and be on his way.

He became aware of a sultry, sandalwood fragrance to his left. He turned and gazed into the blazing green eyes of a woman with flowing red hair who had taken a seat next to him. She wore a pink striped black business suit accented with purple elbow-length leather gloves. Pink lipstick outlined her sensual mouth. Freckles dotted the pale skin of her face. Her wide cheekbones and subtly concave cheeks gave her the look of a European aristocrat. She sat with perfect posture on the bar stool, long shapely legs showcased in sheer purple stockings propped on the brass railing near the floor. She continued to stare at him without saying a word. Light danced in her eyes, as if they absorbed energy from every light source in the room.

Devon smiled at her. She smiled back, revealing a perfect set of brilliantly white teeth. Her open expression told him that she wanted to talk. "I'm not used to seeing gloves in the middle of summer, but they're lovely and compliment your suit beautifully."

"Thank you," she said, extending her hand. "Mathilde de Roche is my name."

Devon picked up a slight accent in her voice. He introduced himself.

"You're a man of good taste yourself," she said, regarding his double-breasted Versace business suit. Devon had recently taken to wearing silk handkerchiefs in the breast pocket. Tonight he wore gold to accent the navy suit. It made him feel less like a bean counter—more his own man.

"I hear some French in your background. Are you from Canada or France?"

"I went to University in France. Do you speak French?"

"Studied it for eight years. Don't speak a word."

Her lips smiled but not her eyes. Those eyes...they were magnetic.

"Most people have to live in a country to learn how to speak the language," she said.

"That's what I tell myself to keep from feeling stupid."

The bartender came back with Devon's bottle of sparkling water wrapped in a plastic bag. "Put it in your gym bag before you leave. I don't want to lose my job." She winked again. Under different circumstances, Devon would have asked for her phone number in exchange for his business card.

He turned to Mathilde. "Care to join me in a glass of innocent refreshment?"

"Thank you. I'm actually quite thirsty."

"I think it must be the summer heat and humidity. I'm parched. Can we have two glasses?" he said.

The bartender glanced briefly at Mathilde and frowned. Reaching up and pulling two glasses from the overhead rack, she set them down on the bar. She left abruptly when another customer called to her from the other end of the crowded bar.

Devon poured the effervescing water into both glasses.

"What a coincidence, the two of us being so thirsty and meeting like this," Mathilde said, raising the glass to her lips.

Devon raised his glass. "To the eradication of thirst." He downed the sparkling water in a series of greedy gulps. His eyes watered. He felt slightly embarrassed. "I don't usually drink like a dry cocker spaniel," he said. "It's just that, well, I can't remember the last time I felt this thirsty."

"You're forgiven. I'm unusually thirsty myself, but I don't think it's from the heat."

Was there a sexual innuendo in her last statement, or was it just his overactive male ego? Then it dawned on him: Mathilde was a Working Girl. She had to be a very expensive one at that.

Her smile disappeared, almost as if she had read his mind.

Somewhere deep in the subterranean bedrock of his subconscious, a faint alarm sounded. He paid no heed to the distant warning. Something about this woman excited him. He liked her poise and self-confidence. Was it real or manufactured? He had the strangest feeling that she knew him — maybe not his deepest secrets; but much better than a total stranger could possibly know him.

Devon poured himself another glass of Perrier. He offered the bottle to her, but she shook her head. After a few more gulps of the refreshing water, he wiped his mouth again. His monstrous thirst began to abate. *I must look like a thirsty diabetic to her*, he thought self-consciously.

She continued to look directly at him. What was going on behind that lovely gaze? He felt, for a second, like he could fall into the depths of her eyes — just sit and look at her beautiful face, into the depths of her luminous eyes, without speaking for hours. She would politely excuse herself and leave if he continued to stare at her like a teenager.

"What do you think of the disappearances?" Devon inquired to change the subject.

"I don't pay that much attention to them."

Mathilde's response surprised him. It was odd, to say the least.

At the age of twenty-eight, with good looks and a five percent body fat ratio, Devon ranked at the top of the list of the local endangered citizenry.

"I don't want to scare you, but we both fit the profile of the people who've gone missing. Aren't you at least a little concerned for your safety?"

"I can handle myself," Mathilde said.

In the past six months, Devon had undertaken uncharacteristic measures to avoid becoming a victim. The 22-caliber sub-compact pistol strapped to his belt shared equal importance with his wristwatch and smart phone. He stole one hour a week from his busy schedule to practice shooting, despite his lack of history with guns or any particular affinity for them. His upper-middle-class parents encouraged education and sports. Criminals, and barbarians carried guns, not upwardly mobile Jewish men.

Times had changed.

Before a twenty-five year-old fitness instructor named Donna Longren had disappeared, Devon fit the accountant stereotype of a

mild-mannered creature with little use for firearms. Nine more people vanished after Donna; all of them from the South Florida area;
one per month. Who was next? The tragedy of the missing persons
had radically altered Devon's self-defense perspective.

The disappearances baffled and frustrated the authorities. The
media sensationalized the story and cried for action. Someone (or
something) had removed ten young professional men and women from
the face of the Earth without a trace of evidence or explanation. UFO
abduction stories from whackos and dark humorists circulated on
the Internet. Talk shows speculated about the identity of the culprit.
Police departments fielded calls from frightened citizens describing
monsters and aliens roaming the streets. The mystery held the population of South Florida in a thrall of panic and fear.

Most of the young professional people Devon spoke with took
the disappearances seriously. His friends tended to stay in groups
when they went out on weekends. Some, like him, bought guns to
protect themselves. Others took up martial arts.

"Do you own a gun?"

"I don't like guns."

"Are you trained in martial arts?"

"Are you worried about me?" Mathilde asked with a sly smile.

"I don't mean to pry. It's just...someone as beautiful as you should
be careful. The abductor chooses good-looking victims."

No blush, no "thank-you" for the compliment: only a slight look
of disappointment.

"Have I offended you?"

Her light laughter sounded like a wind chime. "I don't take of-
fense when a handsome man calls me beautiful."

She looked away, perhaps to conceal a blush, or possibly to signal
her waning interest in the conversation.

He usually read people using his intuition, observing body language and facial expressions, and listening carefully to what they
said. With Mathilde, he couldn't get past the first few sentences of
Chapter One.

The challenge of unlocking a few of this fascinating woman's secrets kept him asking questions. "What do you do?"

She turned back to him and said nothing. He thought it was time to excuse himself and leave the bar until she finally said, "I'm a painter."

"Is there a gallery in town where I can see your work?"

"I don't sell my work. I do it for the pure passion and feeling of accomplishment it gives me."

"How do you support yourself, if you don't mind me asking?

"I do mind you asking."

The Call Girl scenario popped into his head once more.

"I'm not a prostitute," she said without a trace of indignation or judgment.

"You're either incredibly good at reading people or reading minds." He meant it as a joke, but she took the question seriously.

"Do you believe in mindreading?"

"No. What brought you to Miami?"

"Love," she said.

She had a husband or a boyfriend. Maybe she had just broken up with someone. Whatever the case, he decided not to get in the middle of it. Tax season was not the ideal time for a complicated relationship. Truth be told, he never had the time or desire for complicated relationships.

"Well, it's been nice chatting with you. I have to be on my way. Big day tomorrow. Big plans afoot. Have to get my workout in before hitting the sack. Perhaps we'll meet again." *Yeah, like next century. Good luck and have a nice life.*

"Perhaps you'd enjoy your rest better after we've had a chance to satisfy another kind of thirst?" She smiled and finished her glass of sparkling water. "I'm leaving Miami tomorrow. We'll never see each other again. Don't you want to make the most of our time together?"

Her eyes held his in an irresistible embrace. Hit and run. No one gets hurt. What the hell. "Sounds interesting."

"I'm sure we'll find it interesting," Mathilde said, her lips slightly parted. "Shall we?"

www.ingramcontent.com/pod-product-compliance
Lightning Source LLC
Chambersburg PA
CBHW030638110726
47901CB00002B/487